Amethyst

REBECCA LISLE

Illustrated by Paul Hess

Andersen Press

London

For CLEMENCY Beaham-Powell

First published in 2006 by
Andersen Press Limited,
20 Vauxhall Bridge Road, London SW1V 2SA
www.andersenpress.co.uk

Reprinted 2006

British Library Cataloguing in Publication Data available

ISBN-10: 184270 541 5
ISBN-13: 978 184 270 541 4

Typeset by FiSH Books, Enfield, Middx.
Printed and bound in Great Britain by
Bookmarque Ltd., Croydon, Surrey

1

In the Basement

Amy pushed open the front door and paused for a moment on the mat, which did not say WELCOME.

She could hear the thin ticking of a clock. The soft background hum of the freezer and the fridge as they worked overtime.

'Uncle John? Aunt Agnes?'

She didn't call too loudly; she knew where they were, what they'd be doing.

In the narrow kitchen at the back of the house, the freezer door hung open, pouring out cool misty air. A dish containing a grey, gristly-looking stew sat patiently on the thin black cooker beside a pan of grey rice.

Amy piled her books on the table and sat down. She unwound her dark plait, detangling and combing out the thick rope with her fingers.

She sighed.

All day at school she'd had this exciting, niggling

feeling, as if she was about to see someone she hadn't seen for a long time. Or be spiked by a pin. Or someone was going to jump out at her. This certain feeling that *something* was going to happen.

But so far, nothing had.

In Geography she'd had the feeling very strongly, but maybe that was because they were learning about the icy blue Antarctic. She'd so vividly imagined walking over the crisp snow, she'd heard it scrunch and squeak under her boots.

She shivered. There it was again. The feeling! What was it? She spun round. Her elbow caught her pile of books and they slammed to the floor.

CRASH!

She sat very still, listening.

Thump. Thump. Thump. A dull thudding from below made the floor reverberate. Aunt Agnes's high-pitched voice spiked up through the gaps in the floorboards:

'Amy? Amy! Come downstairs and give us a hand, you naughty girl.'

Amy scowled. She'd lost her chance for a few moments peace now.

There was a door, painted to look like part of the wall, below the main staircase. It even had a white radiator stuck on it, so anyone glancing in that direction wouldn't notice it. Amy pushed open the hidden door and plodded down the narrow wooden stairs. She avoided the red brick walls, crusty with creamy patches of mould and free-flowing cobwebs. A bare bulb gleamed dully overhead.

'Here she comes!' Uncle John said.

'About time too, we've not had a moment's break all day and does she care? No.' Her aunt's voice whined like a dying cat. 'She goes galivanting off to her fancy school with her hot friends and leaves us here to do everything...'

Amy turned the bend in the stairs. Her aunt and uncle's faces pivoted round to her. Their pale flesh gleamed with cold sweat. Their skin shone like worm skin. Their pink-rimmed eyes goggled behind thick lenses. Amy couldn't help grinning. Her aunt and uncle looked like giant lobsters beside a rock pool. Their hands held poised above the stone slab table were like massive claws. Everything gleamed in the cold, damp atmosphere, as if a wave had recently rolled over them and left them stranded.

Amy picked up a sharp knife from the table.

'Well, I'm here to help now,' she said.

3

2
The Gargoyles

It was freezing in the basement. Amy slipped her feet out of her shoes so she could soak up the damp cold that seeped up through the vast stone slabs on the floor.

'I have to go to school, you know,' said Amy. 'It's the law.'

'Huh, law!' Uncle John sniffed. 'Laws to say where you park your car. Laws to watch your own TV. Laws for everything.'

'Hurry up and get your overalls on,' said Aunt Agnes. 'We need you. We've got to get this lot fired tonight.' She waved a hand over the grey lumps on the table.

'Here's a pretty fellow,' said Uncle John, winking at Amy. He passed her one of the grey clay lumps from the table. 'I think I've surpassed myself with this one.' He chuckled.

At first sight the shapes looked like a set of distorted giant chess pieces, or grey cats, sitting hunched in rows.

If you looked closer, you saw folded wings, clawed feet and hands. Pointed ears, protruding eyes. Knowing smiles showing sharp and crooked teeth. Gargoyles. They were all gargoyles. The sort of horrifying monsters that leer down from the gutters and half-hidden angles of certain churches.

'Do get a move on spoiling, Amy. There's a whole batch there ready for your final touch,' whined Aunt Agnes. 'Amy, go on. I want to be upstairs by five when the light's gone.'

Amy examined a lump of grey clay. It was a goblin gargoyle with a pointed nose and a humped back. His legs were folded beneath him, so his knees were alongside his ears. His eyes were blank, round and staring. He didn't have much expression yet. That was Amy's job. *She* made them horrible.

'How about I make him nice for a change?' said Amy.

'Don't be silly, girl. Get on with it. I'd do it myself, only I can't make them nasty the way you can. You've got the knack, you know you do. Spoiler. You can spoil anything!'

Amy gulped. Yes, she thought, such a talent for spoiling. For spoiling my friendships, my work, my life. Thanks, Aunt Agnes.

Amy studied the gargoyle's face through half-shut eyes, then quickly reached for a sharp silvery instrument. She began to dig and gouge at his features. She made his eyebrows glower, his eyes gleam with malevolence and his nose grow hooked and mean. She made his shoulders hunch over. His scrawny fingers

5

began to grip his knees as if he was waiting, about to leap. Even his wings grew soft and leathery, as if ready to unfurl and take flight.

'Lovely, lovely!' said Aunt Agnes, taking the finished gargoyle from her. 'Oh, look at him, John! Very unpleasant. You're really got the gift, our Amy.'

Amy did the same to all the gargoyles her aunt and uncle had made. She twisted smiles so they were full of malice. She made eyes glint as if evil ideas lurked behind them. She could change the mildest-looking goblin face into a ferocious frightening monster.

At last they had finished. They carried the gargoyles to the kiln to bake them hard. The kiln was in another part of the basement, protected by a brick wall to keep the heat from seeping out into the rest of the house.

'Just gone five o'clock! Up we go!' said Uncle John. He turned out the cellar lights.

Amy hurried ahead, drawing the snowflake-patterned curtains against the last of the daylight. Soon the house was as bleak and dimly lit as a cave. This was how Aunt Agnes and Uncle John liked it.

The entire house was specially modified for them. The walls were cleverly painted to look like marble with streaks of blood-red, purple and blue over a grey background. The sitting room was painted ice white. A white that gleamed as if it were wet. The room was so cold, that even in summer you could see your breath. A fire seemed to flicker there on the damp winter nights, but it was only pretend: it was red and orange lights and a fan that blew out subzero temperatures.

They ate the gritty, tasteless stew at the kitchen table. No one talked.

No wonder I don't have friends, thought Amy, forcing down the stew. Who'd ever want to come to this place? She remembered her friend Jill whom she'd once invited back for tea. Aunt Agnes had sat her in front of the open freezer and given her iced tripe to eat. She never came again. Surprise, surprise!

After supper Amy went up to her room.

She lay on her narrow bed and stared at the icy blue ceiling.

What had happened to her promising day?

Why did I have that prickling, tingling, any-minute-now sensation, if nothing's going to happen? she thought. Why? Why? Why?

But then something did happen.

3
The Strange Visitor

It began with a noise. A peculiar, scratching, gnawing noise.

Amy sat bolt upright and stared round.

Nothing to see. But, *scritch*, *scratch*, *scuffle*.

Amy pulled her knees up under her chin. She fixed her eyes on the wall where she thought the sound came from. Mice? No, this sounded bigger than mice. A bird? She glanced at the chimney. No, it had been bricked up long ago.

Suddenly, with a ripping, splintering sound, a small section of the skirting board burst out in a shower of wooden shards. An instant later, a large white rat flew from the hole and skidded across the smooth lino towards her.

Amy bit back a scream.

This is it! This is it! she thought. My something!

Little pin-pricking tingles ran up and down her skin. Her throat tightened. Her heart pumped overtime.

The white rat slid over the floor. It crashed into the table leg with a thud. It cleared its head with a quick shake and looked around the bedroom. As soon as its little pink eyes lit on Amy, it smiled. It had neat white teeth. It began to peer around the room; Amy realised it was planning to come up onto her bed.

The rat scrambled onto her abandoned school bag. It sniffed at a bit of toffee stuck to the top of it, then jumped onto the chair. It climbed up the back of the chair and leaped onto the table. It scooted across the table, feet slipping sideways as if it were on a skating rink. Then it jumped onto the linen basket and from there to the bedside table. With a final leap it plopped onto the pillow beside her.

Amy shrank back nervously.

The rat stared at her. 'Pss pss, squeak,' it said meaningfully.

'What? What is it?'

'Pss pss, squeak.'

When Amy shrugged, the rat looked rather annoyed. It began to leap about in a most peculiar way. It twisted and jumped. It did a somersault. It did a backward flip. Finally, with no response from Amy, it lay down flat on its back. It had a very fat tummy. Amy now saw that tied round the rat's waist was something like a small single cigar tube. It was white, just as white as its fur, and therefore almost invisible.

The rat smiled and lay still. Amy reached out and gingerly took the cannister from the belt. The moment she had it, the rat jumped up onto all fours. 'Pss, squeak.'

It flew off the bed, missed the linen basket and landed heavily on the chair. It turned back to wink at Amy, as if to let her know it wasn't hurt, then jumped down to the floor. It skidded across the floor, nails scraping over the lino and bumped against her school bag. It pumped its feet against the smooth surface to regain position, aimed for the hole in the skirting board, shot through it, and was gone.

Amy let out her breath, which she didn't even know she'd been holding in. She listened, head on one side, for any signs of life in the corridor outside. Nothing. Good.

She examined the tube.

It was made of thin white metal, so thin, it felt as if it would easily shatter, but when she squeezed it, it was hard like steel. Etched into the metal were these words:

FOR THE ATTENTION OF AMETHYST
FROM: GRANITE

Amethyst? thought Amy. A mistake. But she knew it was for her. The rat had known it was for her and Amethyst was such a nice name. Not that different from Amy. It *had* to be for her. But why should Granite write to her? He was, as far as she knew, just some guy who bought the ugliest gargoyles from her aunt and uncle.

She unscrewed the top and shook out a letter written on thin, almost see-through paper.

Dear Amethyst,

Greetings from the Lord of the Rock People.

Yes, your Lord, as you are stone and grit and rock as ever there were such things.

It has long been my intention to get you back to the land of your birth, but your aunt and uncle have needed you in their work. I know this. But now I need you and a Rocker does not ignore a call from her Lord.

Come to me at Malachite Mountain. Without delay. There is work to be done. Work which will make you rich.

No school.

No gargoyles.

Rich.

G

Amy read the letter several times then lay back on her bed and stared hard at the ceiling. This is what she'd been waiting for! Malachite Mountain and Granite.

And he hadn't got her name wrong.

She suddenly knew, without a doubt, that her real name was Amethyst.

Uncle John and Aunt Agnes sat opposite each other at the narrow kitchen table, clutching their mugs of iced water and staring deep into each other's eyes. It was breakfast time and they had just heard Amy's news.

'Well, Agnes!' Uncle John rubbed his eyes behind his spectacles. 'Fancy Granite writing to our Amy like that!'

'It's not fair,' wailed Agnes, softly. 'It's not fair. It's not as if we don't provide him with as many gargoyles as he wants for Malachite Mountain. He's jealous. Oh, John, what'll we do?'

Amy gripped the table, hard. All night she'd been imagining this moment, rehearsing what to say. They had to let her go. They had to!

'You'll manage without me,' she said.

'No, but we won't,' said Aunt Agnes. 'There's only you that can put that touch of horribleness onto everything. Only you that's got the fingers for foulness and unpleasantness. We'll never be able to sell our gargoyles if they look friendly.'

'You could learn to spoil.'

'No, but we won't,' said Aunt Agnes. 'I don't think you should leave us. I think you should stay and do your duty.'

I've done it. For years, thought Amy. Let me go!

'Granite is the Lord of the Rock People, which is us all,' said Uncle John. 'We have to obey.'

'Oh, phooey!' said Aunt Agnes. 'What's he to us, now we're safe in the South? He's only Lord of Malachite Mountain because he says he is – he used to be Lord of some little place in the Marble Mountains. I liked that Lord Lazulite, personally. Shame he upped and died so sudden.'

Uncle John took off his spectacles and polished them on his dressing gown. 'It's just a bit of a shock. But we'll have to get used to it, Agnes, dear. Maybe we should all go,' he added. 'I mean, after all, we belong up there, not down here in this infernal heat.'

12

Amy bit her lip. She didn't want them to come. They'd spoil everything.

'No, but no,' whined Aunt Agnes. 'I couldn't leave this house! My lovely brown lino and my new net curtains. Anyway, it's boring up there and you get bossed around.'

'I know, but—'

'And I'm settled here, John, I like my TV and up there is so, so . . . well, so old fashioned. That's why we left, if you remember.'

'I know—' He paused. He rubbed at his head as he tried to puzzle out what was to be done. 'Then Amy will have to go on her own. And Amy, when you get this fortune Granite's on about, you'll have to send us our share. For lodgings and such, all these years we've had you. It's the law you know.'

Amy tried to hide her smile. Good. She could go.

'Tell me about Malachite Mountain. What's it like?' she asked.

'Lots of snow,' said Uncle John.

'And ice,' said Aunt Agnes. 'Lovely. But no supermarkets. Or schools. No cars. No electrics. No TV. No lino.'

Amy's spirits began to soar. 'No school?'

'No. There isn't time for school. Rockers are so busy digging out metals and precious stones. It is more lively down here, I must admit.'

'And it's so far from everything,' said Aunt Agnes. 'And you can't get good white tripe or quality pigs' trotters.'

'Can't you?' Amy almost squealed with delight.

13

'And it snows all the time,' said Uncle John. 'All the time.'

'Well, it sounds horrible,' Amy lied. 'But I think I'd better go. I mean, I can't disobey Granite, can I? I wonder why he wants me? What can *I* do?'

'Perhaps he wants you to spoil something,' said Aunt Agnes, craftily. 'He'll know how good you are at that. Yes, I bet he wants you to do something mean and destructive!'

'He's not a good man,' said Uncle John in a low voice. 'He's bad inside and it shows on the surface – he's as bent and warped as a bit of twisted iron.'

'Once he was in love, wasn't he, John?' piped up Aunt Agnes. She hugged herself. 'He was so in love with that Wood person, that Amber, that he locked her up in a block of ice for years and years and nobody could get her out.'

'And he *loved* her?' asked Amy.

'Oh, yes, very much. It was romantic. But she escaped. Went to live with the Wood Clan.'

'Yuk!'

'Revolting,' agreed Aunt Agnes. 'We heard all about it, though we lived down here.'

'But you used to live up there?'

'We did. We're all Rockers, aren't we? We lived in a mountain near Malachite itself.'

'Granite left the Marble Mountains after Amber escaped,' Uncle John said. 'There was a big to-do. The Wood people were involved.'

'And a bit later on, we started delivering such ever-so horrid gargoyles for him.'

14

Amy hadn't ever heard of the Marble Mountains or Malachite Mountain before. She was greedy to hear more. Aunt Agnes looked at her narrowly.

'You'll find out, soon enough,' she said. 'And I don't think you'll like it!'

'I'll tell him you're coming, then,' said Uncle John. 'School can go to the blazes. You get on working with the gargoyles. It'll be the last chance you have. Agnes'll have to try and copy your style, I suppose.'

'I'll never get it, not that way of making things so bad that our Amy has,' moaned Aunt Agnes.

'Don't worry,' said Amy, jumping up from the table. 'I'll make this batch the ugliest, most malicious, spiteful and revolting that there's ever been. But, just one thing,' she added. 'Amethyst? Is that my real name?'

Aunt Agnes snorted. 'Real? Well, it's the name you were born with, but it's too fancy and flighty for a plain Jane like you.'

'My mum must have thought I was an Amethyst,' said Amy, quietly.

'Yeah, well, she was a flighty, fancy girl, my sister,' said Aunt Agnes. 'And she's dead. No, you stick to Amy and even that's too pretty for someone with such spoiling fingers as yours.'

Amy didn't say anything. But she thought lots.

When I get away from here, she thought, the minute I get away from here, I'm going to be Amethyst for ever and ever!

15

4
Leaving

Amy worked all day in the basement, helping to get the last batch of gargoyles ready. She carved and moulded until her fingers were sore and her eyes stung from the close work. Her thoughts weren't on the job, though, they were flying ahead to Malachite Mountain, to snow and icicles and cold blue waterfalls. She saw herself seated beside Granite (who had become very young and rather good-looking in her mind). They had matching gold thrones. Her fingers dripped with rubies and diamonds. Her thick black hair was tamed, coiled and elegant.

'Give him warts on his nose!' snapped Aunt Agnes, jolting Amy back to reality. 'Concentrate, girl. Make him evil! Granite likes them as ugly as can be.'

'Why?'

'To stop them from wandering. Keep them tied down.'

'*Wandering*—?'

'Never you mind.'

'But what do you mean?'

Uncle John came in. 'Here we are. Train ticket for Amy Basalt. One way only. North.'

Amy grabbed the ticket. She studied it feverishly. There it was: freedom, a new life. The ticket trembled in her fingers.

'Train leaves at eight tonight,' he said. 'It's a sleeper. Arrives tomorrow afternoon at a place called Schist. That's where you get off. It's the last stop. No trains go as far as Malachite Mountain. You're to get off the train and wait there until someone comes for you.'

'Nervous?' asked Aunt Agnes, peering at her.

'No.'

'You should be.'

'You'll need these,' said Uncle John. He handed her a roll of brown cloth.

'What's that? You haven't bought her something, have you?' said Aunt Agnes.

Amy unwound the cloth. It was a short apron. It had ten long pockets with flaps, like envelopes, on the front. Nestling in the pockets was a set of beautiful steel instruments for carving and working stone. It was the first gift that Amy had ever received from her aunt and uncle. They didn't celebrate birthdays or Christmas.

'Don't want Granite thinking we don't look after you,' said Uncle John. 'And it'll mean you can work anywhere, anytime. Might come in handy.'

'And you'll have to work, my girl, you'll see,' said Aunt Agnes, gleefully. 'It won't be a picnic up there in Malachite Mountain, it'll be hard graft.'

Amy didn't say anything. She wouldn't let her aunt spoil things. She was happy. It was the first time in years and years she remembered feeling so good. Nothing was going to alter that.

Her uncle took her to the station. He wouldn't wait for the train. 'You know I don't like crowds, Amy,' he said. 'All this pushing and shoving and the noise and the heat. It's not nice or healthy.'

He handed her her suitcase and melted back in the crowd.

Amy found her seat. She was sharing the sleeping compartment with three other people. They were all women and although they chatted together and smiled at her, she avoided looking at them.

She stared out of the window until it was so black that all she could see was her face reflected back at her. When the train guard came along and turned the seats into bunk beds, Amy was the first to crawl into hers. She turned her back on the others and closed her eyes.

Amy was amazed to find it was morning when she woke; she had slept right through the night. She had also slept through the departure of her three travelling companions. She was alone at last.

Amy turned off the heating and opened the window to let in some cool air.

She looked at the passing countryside. It was wonderful to see fields and forests. She took her new toolkit out. Uncle John had given her a small round stone to carve. It fitted perfectly into her palm. She would

18

make a head. Ahead with the fiercest, most awful face that anyone had ever seen. She set to work, digging and smoothing and sawing at the stone. The jolting train shook her carving so much, she had to hold it hard against her knees. Amy concentrated so intently that she didn't notice the landscape outside slowly changing from green to grey and then to white. When the sun suddenly pierced through the dirty windowpane so brightly she had to put up her hand to shield her eyes, she looked up.

She was amazed.

Outside had completely altered. Everywhere was snow. Everything was white and the white was startlingly bright. The snow sparkled with a million dots of light as it reflected the sun. Beneath the shadows of the trees and in the shade of the rocks the snow was blue or purple or even black.

The train sped past frozen lakes, flat and reflective like giant mirrors; past frozen waterfalls hanging like green and turquoise glass chandeliers. It swept past forests of pine trees weighed down with snow on their branches like dollops of whipped cream.

The distant horizon wasn't houses or hills, but mountain crags reaching far up into the pale blue sky. It was vast and empty and beautiful.

How could Aunt Agnes and Uncle John not have wanted to be here? she wondered. It was perfect.

At last the train came to Schist. She stepped out into a completely white landscape. Her breath clouded in front of her face. The cold air tingled her skin.

'*Wheeze!*' cried the train. Amy jumped out of the way

19

as it retreated slowly, going back the way it had come. The train rails continued for twenty metres then hit a bank of snow. It was the end.

The snow had been brushed aside to form a path. Amy followed it, trying to see over the high banks of snow. There didn't seem to be a ticket office or station, or people, just snow. Once the rattling train had slipped away, there was total silence. The sort of silence that hits you in the face.

She thought she could make out a gateway of some sort, though everything was so covered with snow, it was hard to tell.

It was cold. A cold like no other she'd experienced. It penetrated her flesh like iced needles spiking through her skin to her bones. She undid her thick coat, took off her woolly hat and let the freezing air in. Delicious.

What if they've forgotten me? she thought. Maybe Uncle John had given Granite the wrong information about the train, or which day, or—

Something leaped out in front of her. Amy screamed.

'Gargoyle!'

The squat creature was the ugliest thing Amy had seen. His skin was a dingy blue. He had a large head with massive ears, goggly eyes and a big mouth full of sharp green teeth. If he had wings, they were folded under his jerkin and she couldn't see them. His spiked tail curved out behind him.

'I am a rockgoyle,' said the thing, smiling greenly. 'Welcome to Schist.'

'You gave me a shock.'

He grinned.

He was *so* ugly. Repulsive. Amy suddenly wished she had never made such horrid faces on the clay gargoyles for her aunt and uncle. She felt as if she had made this thing, this creature. 'What's your name?' she asked.

'*This* rockgoyle. *That* rockgoyle. *You* rockgoyle. That's all we are. This! That! You! We aren't supposed to have names or feelings. Come. I'm to take you to Granite.'

Meekly, Amy followed him.

She was disappointed when she saw her transport. It was a small sledge. It had thin metal runners and only one torn leather seat. Not what she was expecting from the Lord of the Rock People. Nothing to pull it either.

'I pull,' he said, reading her thoughts. 'Get on. Put your bags on the end there.'

She did as he told her. She sat down and wrapped a fur rug over her. 'You must be very strong,' she said tentatively.

The rockgoyle took the ropes over his head and settled the leather band across his chest.

'Strong and ugly. Yes.'

He yanked at the sledge and it slid smoothly across the packed snow behind him. He set off.

Amy shrank nervously under the fur cover. A rockgoyle! Yikes! She fixed her eyes on the back of his head, daring him to do anything dreadful. He had a thick, muscular neck. The tendons and ligaments stuck out like tree roots beneath the blue skin as he pulled. His ears were pointed and rubbery and looked as if they had

21

been borrowed from another, larger monster. He wore peculiar leathery clothes, tattered and well-mended.

What if he means to kidnap me? Eat me? Lock me in a dungeon?

Then Amy noticed that he had tucked his tail out of the way, stuffing it into the pocket of his trousers. Suddenly he became less threatening.

The sledge skidded along smoothly. She could lie back against the cushions. She was snug. This is the way it's going to be from now on – except when I'm rich my sledge will be ornate and made of silver and gold. I'll have silky white fur rugs and a whole team of ugly old rockgoyles to pull me along...

Her only worry now was Granite.

5
Granite

The light faded; the surroundings blurred. The shadows crept up closer. Blackness seemed to nudge at her elbows.

'It's awfully dark...'

'Yeah,' said the rockgoyle.

Instantly the sledge began to glow and gleam like moonlight. The snow became tinged with silver.

'Special night metal,' the rockgoyle said. He leered at her over his shoulder. 'Glows in the dark, see.'

'Cool!' She tugged at her cushions, plumping them up more comfortably. 'Are we nearly there?' She had cramp in her knees. She was hungry and tired. All the excitement she'd felt before had drained away. 'We've been going for ages.'

'Not far. We're on the lowest slopes of Malachite Mountain. His Nibs lives at the very top.'

The landscape was monotonous and the rockgoyle was a poor companion. Amy slept.

She awoke to the sound of a bell clamouring. The rockgoyle was tugging on a bell pull beside a vast white door in the wall of the ice mountain. Slowly the door opened. Yellow light spilled out.

'In we go,' said the rockgoyle. He helped Amy off the sledge. He took her bags inside. Amy followed.

She stepped into an enormous cavernous hall lit by hundreds of candles. The floor was shiny marble. The walls glistened with rich veins of silver and turquoise and gold – like home, she thought, but grander.

The rockgoyle showed her into a room on the side. 'Deception Chamber,' he muttered.

'What?'

The rockgoyle was already shuffling away. '*Reception* Chamber,' he said gruffly.

Amy decided the cold had frozen her ears.

The room was very fine with six tall shuttered windows and a marble floor so smooth it was like walking on glass. There was a long metal table with elaborate iron chairs. A candelabra the size of a piano hung from the ceiling; it held at least seventy candles. There were massive paintings of purple mountains on the walls. There was also a grubby outline on the wall where a painting had recently been removed. The plaque beneath it was still there: *Lord Lazulite*. He had been the Lord of the Rockers before Granite. Probably a painting of Granite would soon be hung there, she thought... Maybe one day, a picture of me?

Near the fireplace, there were three large sofas and some plush red chairs around a low, purple stone table.

The chairs and sofas looked unused. In a black cabinet on one wall there was a collection of precious stones, chunks of gold metal and gleaming crystals.

Beautiful, she thought. And no lino. I like it. I like it lots.

Two small, pale-skinned men came in. They had long dark hair and black beards. Rockers. Uncle John must have looked like that before he moved to the South, Amy thought. Weird!

They stood either side of the door. 'Lord Granite!'

Amy held her breath. Please let him like me, she thought. Please let him want me to stay.

There was a shuffling noise, as if some animal like a badger was coming, and a small man waddled in. He was almost bent double, as though caught in a spasm of pain. He looked like a tortoise, the way his head emerged from his curved back. His grey hair was greasy and thin, draped over his shoulder in rat's tails.

'Amethyst! Amethyst! Welcome to Malachite Mountain, my dear,' he said. His voice was rough and gritty. It sounded as if his throat was blocked with rock dust.

He came closer. His skin was ingrained with black. His fingernails were rimmed with black too, as if he'd soaked each one in ink. The word *GOLD* was tattooed across one of his cheeks and over his knuckles, one letter per finger.

'Pleasant journey?' He directed her to sit in one of the soft red chairs. 'I trust the rockgoyle didn't alarm you? But maybe it wouldn't. You're used to that sort of thing, aren't you?' He patted her arm. 'You'll like it here. You

25

can have everything you want. More than your stingy old aunt lets you have, eh? Rockgoyles to do your bidding. Any food you require will be brought to you. I've made up the finest chamber. I have brought you new clothes, fine white furs and pale blue wool. I thought they'd suit your colouring – I was right.'

Amy wasn't used to compliments. She blushed. '*Face like a ferret. Ugly little orphan,*' she heard Aunt Agnes say in her head.

Her heartbeat raced. Granite did like her. Granite was older and uglier than she had expected, but he liked her. He was rich. All those daydreams she'd had when she was tiny, all those stories she'd made up about really being a princess, were almost coming true.

Three rockers came in with trays of food for her. They placed them on the low table, then bowed out of the room.

Nice, thought Amy.

'How are Agate and Jarosite?' Granite was watching her through half-closed eyes.

'Who?'

'Agate and— Oh, ha, ha! You will know them as Agnes and John, I think. They changed their names when they moved South.'

'Agate? Jarosite? Blimey, that doesn't sound like them at all,' said Amy. 'They called me Amy instead of Amethyst, you know?'

'Did they?' growled Granite. 'Here you will be Amethyst. I trust the gargoyle business is going well?'

'Yes.' She could not meet his coal-black eyes as he

studied her. She wanted to like him. He was being kind and attentive, but she felt she was on trial.

'You are perfect for my job,' he said. 'Both sensitive and clever. Just what we need.'

Amy wriggled. 'Thank you.'

'This will be a dangerous mission, but one you are more than capable of, I think . . . The rewards are great.'

'Yes?' She leaned forward eagerly.

'In the valley below the Marble Mountains is a house, a house made out of a Spindle Tree—'

'Ugh,' said Amy. 'I mean, how disgusting. Doesn't it smell? Everything in it must be woody and curved and . . . Ugh!'

'Yes,' said Granite, with a leering smile. 'It is revolting. The people living there are enemies, Wood Clan folk . . . The very ones who drove me from the Rock. It is the girl, maybe not quite eleven, who I'm most interested in.'

Amy nodded.

'She's called Copper.' Granite's voice rattled with emotion. 'I want you to go to Spindle House. Get close to Copper. Pretend to become her friend. Then, when she trusts you, steal her pet wolf cub! Steal it and bring it to me.' His eyes gleamed. He rubbed his blackened hands together. 'Can you do it?'

Amy bit her lip. She was surprised. She'd only ever imagined Granite might want her to do some stone carving. Make special gargoyles. She'd toyed with the idea that he might be searching for an heir . . . a partner . . . but a spy? A thief?

27

She nodded. 'Yes. I'll try.'

'Good, good. Rock solid.'

Amy wanted to ask more questions, but she didn't get a chance. A female rockgoyle with very large hands and enormous floppy ears came to take her up to her room.

'Goodnight, Amethyst,' said Granite. 'Sleep well.' The rockgoyle led Amy up a wide stone staircase to her new bedroom. The room was all sharp angles, rocks jutting out in odd places and a high craggy ceiling. There was an ornate metal bed heaped with silvery furs. A marble bathroom with five mirrors and an onyx bath with gold taps.

An apartment fit for a Rock princess.

Amy watched the rockgoyle closely. Would she really do whatever she asked? Did she really not need a name?

'Hey, you, rockgoyle!' she said, as haughtily as she could. 'Put my bag on that chest. Turn down the bed covers.'

The ugly little creature went very still at first, and Amy thought she was going to disobey her. Then she did as she was told. She was so ugly, with her protruding eyes, big ears and claw-like hands, that Amy found herself sneering at her. 'Ugh, don't touch my things!' The rockgoyle was about to unpack her clothes. 'Go away. I'll manage.'

The rockgoyle shuffled out.

Amy slipped off her boots and socks and stood barefoot on the polished granite floor. She spread out her toes and flattened her feet against the cold, smooth surface.

Bliss.

She padded over to the bed, pushed the heavy furs off and lay down on the crisp white, cool sheets. She gazed up at the jagged, roughly-hewn rock ceiling. She looked round at her splendid room. She smiled.

No wonder Aunt Agnes hadn't wanted her to come here! She was jealous! She and Uncle John would be eating pigs' trotters in their narrow little kitchen! If only they could see me now! she thought.

And they'll have to go on making gargoyles for ever and ever and they'll never be as horrid as mine. Never. And I'll never have to make another one! She drummed her feet on the bed. Brilliant!

Granite was in his room deep inside Malachite Mountain. The room was lined with strips of silver and gold the way ordinary people would line a room with wallpaper. Granite sat at a great slate desk. His chair was carved from finest obsidian and studded with rubies and emeralds. He sipped a turquoise iced drink from a crystal glass.

He was smiling. He picked up the pair of metal knitting needles lying on the desk. He kissed them. Smiled. Kissed them again. A low, gritty laugh escaped his lips. It sounded like gravel slithering down a long, long tunnel.

6

Inside Malachite Mountain

Next morning, after she had been brought her breakfast in bed, Amethyst joined Granite in the Reception Chamber.

'We will go up to the top of the mountain,' Granite said. 'The view is magnificent.'

Amy had no particular wish to see the view, but she guessed Granite was going to tell her more important things. She followed him meekly.

Granite lived in the uppermost third of Malachite Mountain. This meant the rooms, hewn out of the greenish-coloured stone, became smaller and more oddly-shaped, the higher up you went.

'Lord Lazulite dropped dead,' Granite said as they tramped up the stairs. 'Lucky I was available to take command. I was thrown out of Marble Mountain. Discarded like an old boot by my conniving sister and that Copper Beech...Is it any wonder I want revenge, eh?'

The staircase wound upwards like a snail shell. The steps were wide, shallow and well-worn. The floor was a jumble of coloured stone chips, flat and smooth as a skating rink. The landings were lit up by windows of coloured glass. On the walls hideous stone gargoyles were displayed. They were some of the most unpleasant Amy had ever seen – and she'd seen lots.

'Rockgoyles?' she asked.

'Rockgoyles,' repeated Granite.

'Where do they live? The ones that serve us?'

'Down,' said Granite, stabbing his thumb towards his feet.

'I know this sounds a bit mad, and impossible,' Amy said, 'but I – well, some of the rockgoyles look like ones I made, and—'

'Do they?'

'Yes, and—'

But he cut her off. 'More stairs. They've got spiral stairs in that Spindle House,' he said. 'It's a tree. They live in a tree, it's all wood and curves and soft. Pah!'

Wood. A tree house. He'd told her that last night. She was going there. It would be so strange...Being a Rocker, she'd been brought up to despise and mistrust the Wood People.

She didn't dare bring up the subject of the rockgoyles again. It was madness anyway. Probably all gargoyles and rockgoyles looked alike...

Each staircase they climbed up was narrower than the last. They went up in silence, their feet flapping on the hard steps like dying fish.

31

The air grew cooler. Near the top the stairs were less trodden, sharper and harder. They were emerald green. Granite began to puff and grunt. His chest rattled as if it were full of pebbles.

'There are seven flights,' he puffed. 'At the top, crystal. Clear. Magnificent.'

'It sounds fantas—'

'The girl, Copper Beech. The one who owns the wolf cub. She's half-Rock, half-Wood.'

'Really?' Amy stopped. 'I didn't know you could be, but of course her name says it all and—'

'Copper Beech. Huh!'

Rockers and Woods mixing! Immediately a picture of this Copper sprang into Amy's mind. She saw an awkward, misshapen thing with dull brown hair. She was leaning sideways, shifting in the wind. Bending. I bet she can hardly do anything, thought Amy. What *could* such a person do?

'Yes, Wood and Rock,' growled Granite. 'And it breeds disaster, disaster.'

They came out onto a small round landing. The floor was made of shimmering pale stone, like frozen milk, smoother than silk. Granite sat down on a carved stone box.

'Last stop before the crown,' he said. 'See, Copper stole Amber from me. My Amber. She can do it. That's why they took her.' He peered at Amy from below his black brows. 'Amber can make gold... S'true. And you know how? No, course you couldn't imagine it, never. She knits it! Yes.' He paused, breathing heavily. 'She

32

knitted it out of the rock. That's why they took her from me. So she'd make *them* gold.'

Granite stared at the gold rings on his blackened fingers. 'Lovely, lovely gold,' he crooned. 'There whenever you want it. Like a tap. Turn it on. Turn it off—'

'I'd never turn it off!' said Amy.

Their eyes met and they roared with laughter.

'Girl after my own heart!' cried Granite. 'No. Never stop making it, eh? Why would you? And that's why Copper Beech stole Amber from me. For that gold!'

Greedy things! Amy hated them all. Wood People. Enemies.

'Come on, then,' Granite said. He got up. 'One more flight.'

The stairs grew so narrow that Granite's body rubbed the sides as he shuffled along. It was dark. The only light seeping up from the windows on the last landing. Suddenly the stairs stopped. Above Granite's head was a trap door. He pushed it open. Light washed over them like a white tide. Amy was blinded. Granite took her hand and pulled her up into the light.

'The Crystal Crown.'

It was like stepping out on top of the world.

They were at the very apex of the mountain. They were surrounded by a massive crystal globe. It was made from a myriad of glass shapes held together by narrow metal strips, like the mosaic of a giant insect's eye.

'Cazonite Crystal,' said Granite. He sat down on the circular glass bench which ran round the edge of the dome. He waved a hand at the snow-capped peaks and

33

crags which rose up sharp and vivid against the intense blue sky. 'All mine. Everything you can see. It's Rock. Solid. *Mine*.'

Amy put her hand against the crystal. It was cold. It was very beautiful. It was see-through and yet full of minuscule silver and gold fragments, like stars.

'That's fossilised insects trapped millions of years ago,' said Granite. 'Fine stuff, isn't it? There's the odd diamond and ruby in there too.'

'Really?'

'And amethysts . . . somewhere.'

Amy gazed out at the mountains.

'Why do you want me to steal the wolf cub?' she asked. Granite laughed. 'Ralick is special. I want him. You don't need to know more.'

'But—'

'Listen. My sister – calls herself Ruby – she's in charge of the Rock at Marble Mountain. Ruby wants to trust me, though she knows she shouldn't. She wants Rockers and Woods to be allies. She's persuaded the Beech family of Spindle House to let you stay with them. As if we want to be friends, you see.' He chuckled. 'As if I sit around saying, *let bygones be bygones*.' He laughed. 'You go in and get Copper's trust. Then steal the cub. They'll try and turn you against me, but their sappy words won't touch your Rock soul. I know.'

'I hope I can do it.'

'You can.'

'What do I do when I've got the cub?' Amy asked.

'Bring him back here.'

'On my own? Just like that?'

'It won't be difficult. There's a tunnel – a one-way tunnel. It cuts through the mountain. Those soft, sappy Woodies will find it hard to pass through and if they do, they won't get back. There'll be help at hand... Don't worry your little head about a thing.'

Don't worry my little head. Huh! Amy stared at Granite. Where's he been for the last hundred years? she thought.

7
Princess Amethyst

Amy spent the afternoon padding around the icy corridors and empty chambers of Malachite Mountain. She spent some time in Granite's studio, making a gigantic, gruesome gargoyle with twisted lips and long fangs. It felt good knowing other children were in school.

When she was in her sumptuous chamber that night, she concocted lists of all the things she was going to buy when she was rich. She would introduce electricity to the mountain, bring television and real lights! The whole place needed modernising. And if she wasn't going to go to school, then she needed lots of things to do, maybe a home cinema? An ice rink? Some shops. Why weren't there any shops nearby?

Amy delighted in ordering the rockgoyles about. She asked for sandwiches with twenty different fillings. Iced lemonade. Iced tea. Turquoise tea. Fizzing crystal water. She didn't want any of it, but she loved seeing the rockgoyles staggering up the stairs to her room, carrying trays laden with goodies for her.

Amy thought a lot about her mission. Spindle House became a warped, twisted thing in her mind. Weevil holes spotted its smooth surface. It smelt rank, of rotting fungus and mould. It was full of bendy, tall and nasty-smelling Wood People. Twittering birds perched in the branches. Amber, the gold-making mother, was fat, spiteful and rich. Amy made them all distorted and ugly in her mind, just like she made her gargoyles.

The sound of someone laughing loudly broke into her thoughts. Granite's distinctive chuckle – like cascading pebbles, joined in. Amy wondered who Granite was having fun with. Why hadn't he invited her?

In the middle of the night, she woke from a troubled dream. She lay for a few minutes trying to identify what had disturbed her. Then she heard it. A faint, steady throbbing. The noise came from deep down inside the mountain. It seemed to travel up through the walls, the floor, her bed. It was like the thrumming of a large machine . . . Or an army of men marching.

She knew what it must be. The rockgoyles, deep, deep down in the bowels of the mountain.

Amy had quickly got used to ignoring the rockgoyles. She hardly saw the squat female rockgoyle packing a bag for her journey the next day.

'Is it true you're the one who carves us?' the rockgoyle said.

'What?' Amy jumped. She didn't like the rockgoyle's

tone. She didn't like the rockgoyle talking to her before she'd been spoken to.

'Do you make rockgoyles?' repeated the creature.

'I do! Did! Well, I used to make *gargoyles*.'

'Gargoyles. Rockgoyles. We've heard you make them worse and worse, as bad as you can do it. True is it?'

Amy stared into the goggly eyes of the rockgoyle. The creature had no eyelashes, a squashed piggy nose and pointed ears.

'I might. Why?' she said.

'Just wondered,' said the rockgoyle. 'We wondered if it was you, because if it is, we reckoned...'

'What?'

'Nothing.'

'What? Tell me.'

The rockgoyle fixed her bulbous eyes on Amy. 'Granite says you made some of us.'

'That's crazy! No, you've got it wrong. I made stone *gargoyles* for churches, old monuments and things and—'

'But do you make them for Granite? Specially ugly ones for him?'

'Er, well, some of them were for Granite—' Amy stared blankly into a corner of the ceiling. Her skin felt hot and prickly.

'But you didn't know that Granite throws them in the germinating compost and they come out alive?'

'What? I don't know what you— *Germinating compost*?'

Aunt Agnes had always sent the ugliest gargoyles to

38

Granite. But they were just clay models! It couldn't be true... but if it was, then what about those really evil, malicious ones she'd made? Her heart fluttered.

'Only the worst come here,' said the rockgoyle. 'The compost gives them life—'

'Oh, be quiet! I don't want to hear.'

'I'll keep quiet. Only what you've done's not nice. You keep an eye on the mirror, young lady, that's my advice. Spoilers end up spoiling more than they bargained for...'

'Shut up! Go away!'

The rockgoyle shrugged. She went to the door. 'Spoil things,' she said, 'and you'll end up spoiling yourself. Be warned!'

'Shut up!' Amy flung her shoe at the door just as it closed. Horrid little beast! What rubbish! What lies!

Spoiling. What an ugly word that was. She did not like to think of spoiling and mirrors in the same sentence.

No time to think now. Time to go.

Amy was appointed two stocky rockgoyles to take her to the Spindle House. They both had thick necks, skin like elephant hide and pointed, hairy ears.

I shan't talk to them, Amy thought. Granite should have come with me. It's not right sending me off with – animals!

Amy did not speak to the rockgoyles and they did not speak to her. They ignored her. They pulled her sledge down the steep mountain and over the snowy hills as if she were a rather annoying item of baggage.

They spent the first night in an igloo.

'I cannot sleep in here with you!' said Amy. The igloo only had one room and it was quite small.

The rockgoyles did not reply. They made up a bed for her and went and sat outside. They built a fire and cooked food. They told each other jokes and stories. Amy lay inside listening to them chuckling. It took a long time for her to fall asleep.

At last, in the afternoon of the second day, they stopped on a rocky outcrop and looked down into the valley below.

There was a massive tree: Spindle House.

The tree's bare brown branches made it look like a giant's bony hand, protruding from the snow. Smoke streamed from a chimney. Amy could see some large black birds perched in the branches. The blurred contours of a great lake could just be seen in front of the tree. Surrounding it all, at a distance, was a high wall.

Ugly. Horrid, Amy thought. How will I live there? How will I bear it inside that bendy, wooden thing? All that wood!

Twenty minutes later, Amy was at the door. The lintel above was carved into a beautiful dragon. She leaned against the great wooden doors and knocked as loudly as she could. From inside she heard dogs barking. She was afraid of dogs. Granite had never mentioned dogs, only the wolf cub. Holding her breath, she waited for the door to open.

8
Amongst the Woods

There were voices from inside. The door creaked opened.

'Amethyst?' A very tall man welcomed her with a smile. 'You must be Amethyst! Come in.' His glasses slipped down his long nose until just as they reached the tip, he pushed them back. 'You got here all right? Good, good.'

'Of course it's Amethyst, who else would it be?' cried a girl's voice, and Copper pushed forward.

It had to be Copper, it had to be, because of her mass of coppery red hair. It was like a roaring flame around her head. She came towards Amy with a big grin on her freckled face.

Amy could not help smiling back.

'You must be so cold!' cried Copper, grasping Amy's hand and drawing her in. 'Come in! Come in and get warm – or would you rather be cold? I just don't know! Come! Oh, don't mind Silver,' she added. The large grey

41

dog sniffed at Amy. 'She's ever so gentle and friendly –
even though she's a wolf.'

'*Wolf!*'

'Yeah, but honestly, she's gentle as a lamb.'

Silver's broad back reached almost to Amy's waist. Her
fur coat was very thick, sticking out around her neck in a
feathery, silver-tipped ruff. Her eyes were golden yellow,
rimmed prettily with black, as if she wore make-up.
Nervously, Amy slipped past her and followed Copper.

The kitchen door had bowls of fruit and loaves of
bread carved on it. As they went in, a flock of birds
that must have been quietly roosting on the backs of
chairs and shelves, rose up in a flutter, squawking in
alarm.

'Don't mind them,' said Copper. 'I'm used to it now,
but I found it strange too, at first.'

She helped Amy struggle out of her coat.

Amy smiled tightly. The heat was overpowering. So
were the strange smells of wood, the birds, the cooking.
It was making her feel ill. She felt as if a hundred pairs
of eyes were watching her: birds, wolves, people . . .

They'll see through me. Know I'm a traitor, she
thought. Avoiding their eyes, she looked around the odd
kitchen.

The room was shaped like a wedge of cake, wide at
one end and pointed at the other. A slice of tree. There
was a very long table, a dresser full of green pots, large
cupboards and bookshelves. An old black stove.

She suddenly found herself staring at a boy. He was a
lanky thing with messy hair. She felt her pulse quicken.

He wasn't a Wood, was he? He was pale and dark and rocky. What was he doing in Spindle House? He had a penetrating stare which made her cheeks hot.

'This is Questrid,' said Copper. 'He's a mixture of Rock and Wood too. Like me.'

'Questrid's a funny name.'

'It means hunter,' said Questrid.

'Ruby is his mother.'

'Ruby?' For a second Amy couldn't remember who Ruby was. She got hotter and hotter. Copper and Questrid kept on staring at her. Suddenly the name clicked into place. 'Oh, *Ruby*! Yes, she arranged for me to come and stay, didn't she?'

'And here's my mother. Amber,' said Copper.

Amber. Granite's great love who could knit gold out of rock.

Amy got a shock. Amber did not fit the image she'd invented for her. She was younger and more attractive. She wasn't at all fat and greedy looking. Her thick hair was the colour of a gleaming, freshly-opened conker. She had friendly, happy eyes.

'I'm so pleased you're here,' Amber said. 'Copper has so few friends in the mountains. You must stay as long as you wish and treat this as your home – if you can.'

'I'm Cedar, Copper's father,' said the man who had opened the door. 'Ah, and this is Greenwood,' he added.

Amy blinked and had to take a second look at the identical man who had entered the room. The twin brothers were so alike it was as if there was a mirror in the room somewhere, playing tricks on her.

43

Greenwood nodded at her. He collected a pile of drawings from a shelf. 'Glad to meet you,' he said, then he went out again.

Copper grinned. 'Don't mind him, he's very kind, really. Come on, Amethyst, I'll show you your room. I hope you like it. It's not very big because the branches of the Spindle Tree are a little on the thin side.'

Amy felt as if something horrible – a splinter of wood perhaps – was lodged in her stomach. There was a real pain there. All this tree! This terrible wood. She knew she had a frozen smile on her face. She heard her voice and it sounded strained and awkward. There was absolutely nothing she could do about it. If I'd known what it felt to be a traitor and a spy I don't think I'd have agreed to this, she thought. Why can't they be the way I thought they'd be? Stiff, ugly, mean ...

Amy followed Copper up the creaking spiral staircase to the next floor.

'It's all quite new for me, too,' Copper told her. 'I was living down in the South with my Aunt Ruby. I didn't even know about the Woods or the Rocks until I came here – about five months ago. The mountains are fantastic, aren't they? I just feel so at home here. Before I came, I felt as if I was in the wrong place all the time, trying to do the right thing and never managing. But I didn't know why.'

'Yes,' agreed Amy. 'I understand.'

'Oh, do you? I'm so glad. I knew we'd have lots in common.'

44

Amy had spoken without thinking, but it was true. What Copper described was exactly how she had felt. But how could a girl with Wood blood and a pure Rocker like Amethyst ever share feelings?

The wooden staircase was so different from the cold, hard one which spiralled up the centre of Malachite Mountain. This was like walking on jelly.

'Is everything made of wood?' Amy stared up at the beams on the ceiling. Her fingertips fluttered on the wooden bannister. It felt warm and smooth and strangely alive: like touching a snake.

Copper laughed. 'I expect it's really peculiar for you, but for me it's glorious. Absolutely everything is wood. Spindle House is special. It moves, you know? It can tell things about people. I think it listens and watches and feels...'

'Really?' Amy's smile felt as if it was set in concrete. The girl is mad, she thought. As if wood could do that! It can't listen to me!

At the top of the spiral staircase was a circular landing. The main tree branches forked off it. This made all the rooms oddly shaped, with curved ceilings and curved walls. The floor slanted and some rooms had four or five steps going up or down in them, to incorporate the steep climb of the branches.

'Here's yours,' Copper said, opening a tiny door. 'Mind your head.'

Amy felt Copper beaming happily at her. Why was the wretched girl so merry? 'It's pretty,' Amy managed to say. 'I shall love it here.'

The room was round, with a small arched window set deep into the thickness of the tree trunk wall. The wooden floor and walls gleamed like golden honey. Awful, Amy thought as a wave of nausea swept over her. I'll get claustrophobia. Or woodphobia. I'll be sick. And if Copper keeps grinning and smiling and being so maddeningly nice, I'll die!

Copper pointed to the bed. 'We cut off the legs and replaced them with stone pillars,' she said proudly. 'And there's an iron headboard. Questrid helped make it. He said you wouldn't want to sleep on wood, it might give you a headache. It does to him – or it used to.'

'He's right,' Amy said. 'Even being in here...' She stopped. 'Well, I'll see how I get on. Which is your room?'

'Just here.' Copper opened the next door along the corridor and stood back to let Amy into her room.

'Oh, and this,' she added, waving towards the bed, 'is Ralick.'

9
Ralick

Amy stopped dead. She stared at the scruffy ball of fur on the bed.

'A stuffed toy?'

'My wolf cub.'

Wolf cub! She'd forgotten all about it. The wolf cub she had to steal. The reason she was here. How could she forget?

The little cub uncurled itself. Its fur was darker than Silver's, a soft gold, with white-blond patches round its eyes. A dark streak ran down its forehead and from each eye, joining to make a dark line down the bridge of its nose. It had golden eyes.

'What did you say it was?' she gulped.

'*He*'s a wolf cub,' said Copper. 'He's four months old. He's still got his baby fur, but later he'll be more silvery-coloured. Isn't he gorgeous?'

'Er, yes.'

Then Amy saw a strange thing. She saw Copper and the wolf cub exchange a very particular look. It wasn't just that their eyes met, nothing so simple, no, she was sure. They looked at each other as equals, as friends. As intelligent beings.

Granite was right, she thought. This cub *is* special.

Ralick yawned and stretched. He rolled over so his little pink tummy showed. His out-sized paws hung limply as Copper rubbed his underneath and stroked his head. She fondled his thickly-furred ears and cooed at him.

'I don't know why he's up here. He slipped away when you knocked at the door. I expect he didn't like all the commotion. He's my very closest friend, Amy. I hope you two will get on.'

The way they gazed at each other was sickening. Amy felt herself growing tight and angry. As if some internal spring was being wound up, and was getting shorter and springier and about to burst.

'How sweet.'

'Thank you. He is. Ralick and Questrid are special. And now you, Amethyst. I'm so glad Ruby arranged for you to come and stay.'

Amy smiled weakly. There she goes again, she thought, gushing like a waterfall, and nice. So NICE.

'I'll go and unpack my things,' Amy told Copper.

'Do you want me to help?'

'No, no,' said Amy. 'Thanks.'

She scuttled into her bedroom and closed the door.

She snatched her hand away from the door as she shut

48

it: Yuk! Even the handle was made of wood. It was shaped into an acorn, and so realistic that if it hadn't been so big, a squirrel would have been fooled. She stood very still so the floorboards wouldn't creak, closed her eyes and tried not to breathe the wood smell in too deeply.

It was all so weird. That horrible wolf cub thing, she thought. I hate it. And I hate Copper. Why do they look at each other like that? Secrets. They've got secrets but I'm not jealous. How could I be jealous of a wolf and a Wood girl?

But she was...

All her life her uncle and aunt had drummed into her how plain she was. How stupid. The only thing they'd praised her for was for spoiling things. They'd told her stories about the weak and wishy-washy Wood Clan and the superiority of the Rocks. Now here she was, surrounded by wooden things and Wood People – and it wasn't the way they'd described it at all.

Copper truly seemed to like her. Nobody had ever liked her before. Because how could anyone like her? A spoiler? But Copper didn't know about her spoiling skills...

Amy went over to the window. She needed more air. She felt weak. The effect of Copper liking her was actually making her feel wobbly, as if bits of her were leaking out.

Or was it just being surrounded by all this wood?

She pushed open the window and sucked in the cold, fresh mountain air. She felt better immediately. I must be strong, she told herself. And cold. Like stone.

Amy's room was at the back of the house, over-looking a small courtyard. Two very large horses leaned over their stable doors on the far side of the yard. In the roof above the stable were three windows. Copper had told her Qestrid had that room.

As Amy turned back to the room, she caught a glimpse of herself in the mirror above the chest. She stopped.

She looked different! She stood very still. The rockgoyle's words came back to her. Sharp, agonising, like a dagger stabbing, the words cut her.

Spoiling! Spoiling! You'll spoil yourself!

She leaned closer and studied her face, scanning every inch of it in the mirror. Her nose was bulbous! Her eyelashes were shorter, they definitely were and there were bumps around her chin like warts!

Amy's heart pounded and throbbed painfully. She closed her eyes. She took a deep breath. She wiped the mirror over, bent even closer...

There. Nothing. It was rubbish! She was fine! Just her imagination. Silly. The rockgoyle had been trying to scare her, that's all ...

Someone knocked on the door. Amy jumped and spun round.

'Sorry!' Copper burst in. 'I thought maybe I should help you get sorted because the sooner it's done, the sooner we can go out and I can show you everything – before it's dark. Did you see the horses?' She squeezed in beside Amy, next to the window. 'Thunder and Lightning. Aren't they fantastic? They pull the big sledge. Questrid's in charge of them.'

Amy had to fight to speak normally.

'Is he?' she said. She took a big breath. 'Really. Why doesn't Questrid live in here?'

'Because he likes it out there,' said Copper, leaning against the wall beside her. 'Sometimes Questrid thinks he'll go back to the Rock and live with Ruby, but he doesn't like the Rock – it's ever so stony and gloomy. Oh, sorry again. That sounds rude! Of course it won't seem gloomy to you. Or stony! He likes bits of both worlds. Here, let me get this stuff packed away,' she added. She began tossing Amy's clothes into the drawers.

'I suppose the Rock's not what he's used to,' she went on. 'You do have a lot of clothes, Amy... Questrid didn't know who his parents were. He didn't want to believe he was a Rocker, poor thing, but he carves stone beautifully which is such a giveaway. But now Questrid accepts he's a bit of both. It turns out his father was a Wood. You seem perfectly happy being who you are. I like that.'

Amy swallowed uncomfortably.

'This is going to be such fun!' cried Copper. 'You've no idea how much I've been looking forward to you coming. I've never really had a proper friend before—'

'Not even in the South?' asked Amy.

'No. I felt so different. What about you?'

Amy was caught off guard.

'Oh, lots. Lots and lots of friends,' she lied. 'Yes. I really like my school. I'm in the top set for everything.'

'Wow!' said Copper. 'Well done.'

51

Amy stared at the carved wooden chest without seeing it. 'My friends must miss me,' she added lamely.

'Oh, don't worry, we'll get letters. Bird o'gram. It's very reliable but of course sometimes the letters are a bit pecked . . .'

'Yes?' What an idiot I am, Amy told herself. I don't need to make this up. I don't have to. 'My best friend's called Izzy,' she heard herself rattle on. 'She's very pretty, blonde. Really good at netball.'

'Really? You lucky thing!' said Copper. She sat on the bed. 'At my school everyone laughed at me for knitting.'

'I didn't know you knitted.'

'I did. All the time. Aunt Ruby never minded about me knitting. It's the only thing I miss here. I used to knit when I was unhappy or feeling unravelled and loose. I knitted when I was happy too. I just had to knit. But now . . .'

'Yes?'

'Well, Amber, she's—'

'What?'

'She's *hidden* my knitting needles. Every single one she could find. And my crochet hooks. She doesn't want me to do it any more.' Copper turned her green eyes on Amy. 'Why do you think she did that?'

'I don't know.' Amy leaned forward, hoping Copper would tell her about Amber knitting gold. Did she still do it? Where did she do it? Were they rich?

But Copper only giggled.

'I've no idea why she did it either,' she said. 'She used to like knitting too. Actually, I do still have one little pair that Aunt Ruby gave me years ago.' She grinned. 'I'm keeping them hidden. Just in case Mum gets her hands on them. Have to knit, you know.'

They heard the patter of claws on the floorboards outside and Ralick came in. He sat down at Copper's feet. She stroked his head.

'I don't mean to say anything against your people,' Copper said. 'But Granite kept my mother a prisoner once. And Silver, too. Her babies died, all except Ralick. I'll never forgive him for any of that. He locked me up. He's mad.'

'Oh, yes, well . . . ' Amy wondered what she could say. 'Granite's old-fashioned. He'd like to keep the Rockers and the Woods separate, wouldn't he? He doesn't like mixing.'

'That's right. He lived in the Rock up there.' Copper pointed vaguely out towards the mountains. 'He's gone now. Some people say he killed Old Lord Lazulite to take over his domain. I wouldn't be surprised . . . Now Granite reckons he's the new Lord of all the Rock People. That's what I've heard.'

The cub was staring at Amy. His brow was wrinkled as if he understood what they were saying. It was really very unnerving.

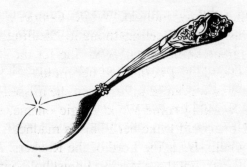

10
Amy's First Meal at Spindle House

Copper showed Amy all over the house, then all round the snow-covered garden. Amy felt brighter outside in the cold air.

Ralick followed them.

'The lake's frozen. Cedar says the ice is a metre thick,' said Copper. She squatted down beside the ice and wiped away the dusting of snow. The water had turned a clotted, hazy grey. 'We can go skating if you want. And we can go sledging later. Questrid's been working on making a sledge for you ever since he knew you were coming.'

'Has he? Why?'

'To make you feel at home of course.' Copper stared at her. 'What a funny question!' Copper picked up Ralick and snuggled him under her chin, kissing the flat top of his head. 'But you can't come, Ralick. You'll have to stay behind.'

Skating. There might be a chance for me to grab

54

Ralick then, Amy thought. While Copper's busy...
But it was only a fleeting thought. Stealing the cub
seemed rather unimportant now. She let the idea slip
back into the deeper corners of her mind.

When Amy was alone in her room she missed Copper.
Copper's working some Wood magic on me, she told
herself. How could I like her? This is madness. Granite
needs my help. *He* is the Lord of the Rockers. *He*'s the
one that counts, not these Woods. I must hold out against
the Woods and all their charms.

She needed to feel something Rocky. She took the
stone carving she had begun on the train from her bag.
She clasped the cold rock between her pale hands. The
face she'd chiselled was only a blur, just a suspicion of
a nose, mouth and eyes, it wasn't revolting – yet.

I could make it nice, for once, she thought. There's no
Uncle John or Aunt Agnes to make me spoil it.

What if this stone was me? I'd want to be beautiful,
wouldn't I? But still hard and strong?

A corner of her sculpture crumbled to dust and fell
into her lap.

At seven o'clock, Copper called Amy to come downstairs for supper.

The kitchen was bright and too warm. Cedar and
Amber were there. A small woman with a long striped
skirt was stirring a pot on the cooker.

'This is Oriole,' said Copper. She led Amy towards
her. Oriole spun round and fixed Amy with her bright,
beady eyes.

Amy noticed immediately the way Oriole put her head to one side to look at her and how she hop-walked like a sparrow. 'You aren't a Wood!'

Oriole laughed. 'No, my dear, I'm from the Bird Clan of course and this is Robin, my husband.'

Robin was also short, with long hair tied in a ponytail. He stood with his arms tucked behind his back like folded wings. A large, startlingly white seagull sat on his shoulder. It snapped its curved beak. Its shiny yellow eyes were like tiny wet berries. They glared at Amy.

'This is Casimir. He's a snow seagull. Don't mind him,' said Robin, cocking his head on one side, just like the bird. 'All show he is.'

Amy tried not to mind him. She tried not to mind any of it: the wood, the warmth, the animals – enormous Silver and little Ralick, tucked up in Copper's arms. Bravely she admired the green and white pots arranged neatly on the dressers. She cooed over a nest of thrushes she spotted tucked in behind a teapot. She tried to ignore the constant traffic of birds swooping around the room and singing all the time.

'I look after the birds,' Robin told her. 'If you're good to them, they'll look out for you. Ask Copper.'

'It's true,' Copper said.

Amy smiled. Inside her head alarm bells rang. Granite hadn't told her everything. Yes, he'd said there were birds, but these seemed different from ordinary birds. Specially the snow seagull. It looked really smart. Any one of them might see me if I – *when* I try to steal Ralick – and they'll easily follow me. I'll have to be very careful.

Questrid came in. Their eyes met and Amy smiled as best she could, but he knew! She could tell! He gave her such a calculating stare. He knew she was a spy. His honey-coloured eyes were fierce and hard as amber. She expected him to leap on her and demand to know what she was up to.

But he didn't. He patted Ralick and then politely asked Amy what she'd been doing and if she liked Spindle House.

'It's wonderful here,' she said.

'But I expect you'd rather live up at the Rock,' said Questrid. He eyed her suspiciously. 'More your type of thing.'

'I've never been to the Rock, never been up to the mountains at all,' she said. 'Though I know it was Ruby's idea. Helping break down the barriers between our clans. Forging new links, that sort of thing.'

'Hmm,'said Questrid. 'Trust Ruby to think this one up.'

The rest of the family came in and took their places at the long table.

Amy noticed that everyone had wooden spoons and wooden-handled knives and forks, except her. Even Amber did, and she was a pure Rocker. Amy had been given a silver soup spoon. It was engraved with flowers and birds.

'It's very beautiful,' she said. 'Far too lovely for me!' She distinctly heard her Aunt Agnes's voice saying: *She'll spoil it! She spoils everything!*

'Oh, that's nonsense, Amethyst. It's perfect for you,'

said Amber, gently. 'Why shouldn't you have the nicest thing? You're lovely too!'

Amy felt her cheeks go so red and hot she thought her head might burst. A compliment. They were so rare. First Granite and now Amber. Amy stared down at the table, waiting for someone to contradict Amber, or laugh. No one did. Conversation continued around her. Amy stared unseeing at the loaf of bread, listening to Aunt Agnes whining in her head: *Don't believe a word of it. You're not pretty. You're as ugly as a gargoyle. Horrible little girl! Glad you're not mine!*

Had Amber only said that to make her feel good? Had she guessed Amy was a spy, a traitor and liar come to steal? Was it a trick to disarm her?

'You could try a wooden spoon if you wanted,' Questrid said.

'Could I? I just feel I ought to do the same as all of you,' said Amy. 'I mean, I'm trying to fit in, aren't I?'

'Sure, go ahead!' Questrid handed her a wooden spoon. He glanced at the silver spoon as he took it away. Amy saw him out of the corner of her eye. He slipped the spoon into his pocket. She felt anxious. The silver spoon had changed, she'd felt it. She'd spoilt it.

Amy picked up the wooden spoon. Everyone else stopped eating to watch her.

Uh oh, she thought. A trick of some sort? They were holding their breath, they were staring! Using a wooden spoon can't be that difficult!

'Go on,' said Copper.

Amy dipped the spoon into the soup, then, as she raised it to her lips, the handle went completely slack. It hung limply from her hand like a rag. Soup dribbled out.

'Ow!' cried Amy, dropping the spoon. 'What the ... ?'

Everyone, except Amber, burst out laughing. 'Don't mind them, or the spoon,' she told her. 'It's a Greenwood spoon and temperamental. So much for our two clans working together, hmm? Stick to the metal one for now, until you've got a bit more influenced.'

Amy hoped nobody could see the tears smarting her eyes. 'But you're a Rocker, Amber,' she said. 'How can you use the wooden ones?'

'Practice,' said Amber, gently.

'And Copper and Questrid,' Amy went on. 'They've got Rock in them ... They can do it.'

'Never mind,' said Questrid passing her a less elaborate metal spoon and hurriedly offering her some bread. 'If you really want to use a wooden spoon it will let you soon enough. Listen! Did you hear that wind? I think a storm's brewing up.'

The conversation about the spoon was dropped. But not forgotten.

Not by Amy.

And not by Questrid.

That night Amy lay in her iron and stone bed unable to sleep. Outside the wind was howling. It whistled and whined as it roared through the branches of Spindle House. The old tree creaked and groaned, bending against the blast. Amy imagined Copper lying snug and warm in her bed, with her arms around the wolf cub, luxuriating in the movement of the tree around her. But poor Amy lay stiffly on top of her covers, too hot to sleep, thinking about steady marble floors and unflinching malachite walls.

When there was a sudden lull in the roar of the wind, she heard the murmur of voices from the next room. She heard Copper's voice, and another voice she didn't recognise. Surprised and intrigued, Amy slipped out of bed and put her ear to the wall. Someone was talking to Copper, but who? It was a gruff, low voice, neither like a child nor an adult.

With a whoosh, the wind suddenly tore at the tree again. It whined through the branches and drowned out the voices. Amy waited a few more minutes, but the wind didn't let up and she went back to her bed, puzzled and thoughtful.

She slipped between the sheets, pushing her toes down to the end where it was coldest. But there was something down there. Something alive.

'Eeek!' She yanked back the covers.

It was the white rat. Amy didn't want to see the rat. He made her think about Granite. She didn't want to think about him or why she was here.

The white rat sat on her pillow. He twitched his nose and whiskers at her. His pink eyes were alight with mischief.

'Pss, pss! Eeek!'

'Hello,' said Amy. 'What do you want? How did you get here? It's miles and miles from Malachite Mountain! Do you have a message there?'

He did. Amy took the small slip of tissue paper from the tube. Her heart beat faster.

Woods tell lies. They have a thick layer, BARK, but it flakes and cracks easily. Beneath it is SOFT SAP and pale wood. Inside that, nothing. Nothing but LIES.
Steal the beast quickly!

Well. Thanks Granite. Short and not very sweet, Amy thought. I wish, I wish – I wish Granite were different. I wish I were different. I wish I were a nice Rock girl and didn't have to do this!

The rat curled up on her pillow and went to sleep.

Amy gingerly laid her head down beside him. Almost like having a pet, she thought. She touched him with her fingertips and stroked his fur. It was so soft. The rat began to purr. Rats don't purr, thought Amy. But this rat did.

Amy wrapped her other hand around the iron bed rails. The coldness seeped into her flesh and soothed her.

Lies. Yes, it was all lies. Granite was right. They didn't trust her so they were being so nice to her, lulling her into feeling safe. She forced herself to picture her room in Malachite Mountain. She saw her icy chamber, the gleaming rock walls and splendid mirrors. She saw all the things she was going to have when she was rich. Fine gowns. Parties. Silver skis. White skates with gold blades...

But as she visualised it, it altered... She saw herself opening a wardrobe full of gowns which were covered

61

in dust. She threw back the doors to welcome people to her party and there was no one there. Her lovely skates lay beside the frozen lake unused. Amy stood in the Reception Chamber with Granite and he was laughing at her...

11
On the Frozen Lake

Next morning Amy looked out of her window. The light was strange. The sky looked bruised, purplish grey, threatening snow.

Questrid and Copper were in the yard stroking the horses' noses and feeding them carrots. Amy dodged out of sight. She tried to catch what they were saying.

'You were mean to her last night. What were you trying to do?' said Copper.

'She's...' Questrid's words were lost in the wind.

'...You must be kind to her...Think of what Aunt Ruby would say...You and Ralick are both...'

Oh, it was so annoying! Amy heard a few words and then the rest were snatched away.

There was a hoarse croak and Amy looked up and saw the big white seagull, Casimir, on the roof opposite. He was staring at her. His yellow eyes fixed on her greedily, as if she were a herring.

'Sssss!' she hissed at him.

Amy closed her window. They're talking about me. The bird's spying on me. It's not fair. They don't trust me. Serves them right that I'll steal Ralick!

I wish they were really nasty, Amy thought. Like Aunt Agnes and Uncle John. But they're not. I'm not used to all these smiles and kind words. And that Amber! She's the worst. She's like a perfect sort of mother, a dream mother from a book. I love her. I hate her!

Amy couldn't help imagining staying at Spindle House. She'd become part of their family, helping them carve wood instead of stone. She saw herself with a wooden figure in her hands. It was lovely – no, it was horrid, it was turning into ugly little goblins with evil expressions... the goblins suddenly came alive! They ran round the house setting it on fire. She could hear Copper screaming.

Amy shook her head. Stop it! That's what sleeping surrounded by wood does to you, she told herself. It's not safe.

The white rat had disappeared again. She wondered if he had stayed all night, or crept away in the dark. She hoped he had stayed. She dressed and went downstairs.

'Good morning, dear,' said Oriole. 'I have a bowl of porridge ready for you. Honey or brown sugar?'

'Honey please,' said Amy, then was cross with herself for not just making do with salt, as she had at home. I'll go soft like them if I stay here much longer.

A blackbird sat on the back of a chair. It cocked his head at her as if about to ask her a question. Suddenly it

64

flew off and disappeared through a tiny gap in the window.

'Don't they make a mess everywhere?' asked Amy, picking up a feather from the table.

'Not more than the odd bit,' said Oriole. 'Robin trains them to be clean in the house, of course.'

Amy finished her porridge, put on her boots and went out into the courtyard. There was no sign of Questrid or Copper.

The sky was very dark. It looked hard and shiny, as if there was a domed metal helmet curving above her head.

She went over to the horses and tried to stroke their noses. They backed away, snorting. Amy kicked the door crossly. 'I don't care,' she said. 'See if I care. I didn't want to stroke you anyway, nasty, big, smelly thi—'

Copper came out of the shadows at the back of the stable. 'What's the matter, Amy? Are you all right?'

Ralick, as usual was in her arms. Questrid followed a few paces behind. 'It's nothing,' said Amy.

'We heard a noise.'

'Just the horses banging against the door.'

Questrid shot her a dark look.

'We've been to get the skates,' said Copper. 'Look. Aren't they fine?'

Questrid dangled three pairs of skates in his hands. 'Hope you're size four!'

'Yeah, sure, something like that.' Amy knew she sounded rude. I must be good-tempered. I must. Remember the money, she told herself. Remember being

65

here means no school. Living up here for ever. Princess-style. Be nice!

'It's still a bit windy, isn't it?' she said. 'Do you think there'll be a storm? The sky's so heavy.' A storm might be perfect, she realised. She could disappear in a blizzard.

'Hope not, but think yes,' said Copper.

They walked side by side to the snow-covered lake. Their shoulders bumped together. When Amy slipped, Copper pulled her up, laughing. When Copper explained something enthusiastically, she slipped her arm around Amy's waist. Amy meant to shrug her off, make her leave her alone. But she couldn't. She liked it. She liked Copper liking her.

'Isn't it cold?' said Copper.

'Not really,' said Amy. 'The colder the better.' She heard herself laugh; the same light-hearted laugh that Copper had. Something was happening to her – she wasn't acting.

Today the frozen lake was violet-coloured, reflecting the strange steely sky. The wind lifted the loose snow and flung it about, whisking and curling and rolling it in flurries. It dusted their heads and clothes.

Questrid put his skates on and set off. 'Yahoo!' he yelled. 'Watch me!'

Amy sat down on the lake edge to put on the skates. I'm trying to hate them, Granite, honestly I am, she said silently. I know I've got to steal Ralick. I know... She looked at Ralick. He was curled up in a hollow beside the lake. His fur was all standing on end, lifted by the wind, like a dandelion clock. She felt her tummy squidge inside her when she looked at him. He looked so sweet...No! No, he doesn't! She looked round guiltily. As if Granite was watching and could read her mind.

'Come on, Amy! What are you dreaming about?' cried Copper. She had already got her skates on. 'Those do fit you, don't they? If not you can have these, they're a bit bigger. The skates we gave you are the newest and fastest.'

Typical, thought Amy. Copper gives me the best ones. Typical.

She kept her face hidden as she did up her laces so they couldn't see her expression. She wasn't sure quite what her expression showed, but it felt odd, confused. It would surely tell them something about her.

Questrid was circling the lake, his long striped scarf trailing behind him.

Copper skated up to her. She grinned and held her arms out to Amy but Amy pretended not to notice and skated straight past her.

Spoil it, spoil it, she thought, spoil it all, Amethyst Basalt, just like you do the gargoyles. Tears stung her eyes. I wish Granite had never thought up this plan. Wish I could be an ordinary girl called Amy with ordinary Copper. Simple. So simple.

They circled the lake several times, getting the feel of the ice. Suddenly Questrid gave a yell. He started to chase them. Amy squealed, she couldn't help herself. She went faster. Questrid zoomed alongside her. He knocked off her hat. He nudged her arm sending her off in a mad whirl. He skated up behind her and shunted her along like a train. Amy laughed out loud. She'd never heard herself laugh like that. It was wild and wonderful. Granite, Malachite Mountain, the rockgoyles, all those things, flew from her mind. All she knew was the wind on her cheeks. The searing sound of her blades cutting the ice as she skidded over the lake.

Time passed. The chance to steal Ralick, if there ever had been one, was lost.

The wind suddenly shifted gear. Now the strong wind pushed against them and slowed them almost to a standstill. Hard pellets of ice, like frozen peas, stung their cheeks. The sky grew darker and heavier. Snow began to fall. Great fat chunky snowflakes whirling about so they could hardly see.

'Time to go in!' roared Questrid. He skated to the bank. 'Oh, look at Ralick! He's turned into a snow-cub!'

The falling snow had almost hidden Ralick. He quickly jumped up and shook it off. He bounced about, tossing the snow with his nose, biting it fiercely. He skidded through a snow heap on his belly and shot out the other side shaking himself.

'He loves the snow,' Copper said. 'Wolves don't mind the cold at all, their fur is so thick. But I do! Let's go in. I bet we'll be stuck inside for the rest of the day now!'

12

The Unexpected Visitor

The storm had arrived. A fierce wind ripped and roared around Spindle House. The tree creaked. Snow fell thick and fast, it drifted against the windows till they were blocked with white.

Copper dug out an old board game called Goblins, Dwarves and Diggers. She put it out on the kitchen table and they tried to work out how to play. They had to shout above the sound of the wind. 'I think you go into the mountain first,' Copper said, 'then you can—'

BANG! BANG! BANG!

Someone was hammering on the front door. The birds lifted, twittering in alarm, then drifted back to their perches.

Silver barked. Her hackles rose stiffly like a scrubbing brush.

Cedar and Questrid went to the door. Silver padded behind them growling.

'Who could it be?' said Copper. 'We *never* get visitors!'

'I'm one, don't forget,' said Amy.

The big door was outlined with light. Something on the other side was shining very brightly.

'What is it?' whispered Amy.

'I've no idea,' said Copper.

'Keep back, Questrid,' said Cedar. He opened the door. At first it looked like a pillar of dazzling, brilliant light on the doorstep. Then Amy saw it was a man. Light oozed out of the pores of his skin. It came through his clothes and even out of his eyes.

'Good evening to you. Good evening,' he called. 'Do excuse the light now, won't you? It'll fade, sure it will.'

He glided into the hall as if blown there on a puff of wind.

He was a small, slender man with silvery hair surrounding a glowing translucent disc of a face. His eyes were pale grey. A white fur cloak was slung over his shoulders. Beneath it, he wore pale floating garments and white boots.

He brushed the snow from his shoulders and hood. 'My name is Shane Annigan, so it is. Thank you for letting me in. Thank you indeed!'

Everyone watched him as he went into the kitchen. The birds twittered and scattered.

Amy stared. Now there was a new outsider which made her an *insider*.

'The wind has blown us *another* visitor,' said Cedar. 'This is Mr Shane Annigan.' He took the man's cape and hung it up. Snow melted and dripped to the floor.

'Come and sit by the fire,' Amber said. 'You must be cold. Are you hungry? Tired?'

Nothing ever upsets or surprises her, thought Amy admiringly. She imagined Aunt Agnes twittering and going into a tizz: *Look at that mess on my clean floor! We don't want your sort here, you light-bulb man! Get off with you!*

Shane Annigan illuminated different parts of the room as he sailed past. He made the kitchen seem dull when before it had seemed bright. He wafted towards the big rocking chair and settled down as gently as a feather.

Oriole handed him a mug of hot chocolate. 'Good evening,' said Uncle Greenwood, who had come into the kitchen to see what the fuss was. He peered over his spectacles at the visitor. 'Greenwood's the name.' He waved a length of half-worked wood at him. 'I was carving downstairs. We rarely get strangers at Spindle House, I had to come and see.'

'Delighted,' said Shane Annigan. He beamed at Greenwood but gave Amy a quick, suspicious look. She had a sudden premonition that he would interfere with her plans. A jab of fear shot through her.

'Have you come far?' asked Amber.

'Far, yes . . .' Mr Annigan took a sip of his drink. He looked round at everyone. 'What a family this is!' He revealed long creamy teeth in a wide smile. 'I am thinking there is both Wood and Rock in this place?'

Cedar nodded.

'A good combination.' His pale eyes glanced from one to the other. 'But, sure, you must be from the Bird

71

family?' he asked Oriole. 'Since you have beady black eyes and are as round and short as a wren – no offence – it's plain as plain.'

'That's right. Not quite family, being from another clan, but close as you get. Robin too.'

Mr Annigan nodded. 'Wood, Rock, Bird all gathered together. I myself, as you might have guessed, am of the Air.'

'*Air!* I've never met an *Air* person before,' said Questrid. 'Do you all shine like that?'

'Not met a man of Air before? Well, well, there's a thing. I come from a long way off and was caught in the blizzard, tossed and tumbled and thrown around like a dandelion seed. How I got here I will never know but I saw your lights and . . . here I am.'

'Lucky you got blown this way,' said Cedar. 'There aren't many houses around.'

'I shall ask him questions all night,' Questrid whispered to Amy, 'and won't let him go to bed till he's told me exactly what it's like to be – a *lantern*.'

Mr Annigan settled himself back in the chair. He sipped his hot chocolate. As he looked around; his eyes cast a small, narrow beam across the kitchen, like a lighthouse. Amy wondered what it was about him that she didn't like. Perhaps he smiled too much.

'Would that be a snow wolf?' Shane Annigan asked Copper. He nodded at Ralick.

'His mum, Silver, she's a snow wolf. We don't know who the father is.'

What was he interested in the wolf cub for? thought Amy. Ralick was hers. And Granite's!

'Where were you going before you drifted to Spindle House?' asked Cedar.

'I was on my way to Dragon Mountain,' said Mr Annigan. He swivelled his silvery gaze round to Cedar.

'Dragon Mountain! Where's that? Why?' Questrid leant forward eagerly. 'Sounds brilliant! I'd love to see Dragon Mountain.'

'It's a long way from here, way past Antimakassar,' said Shane Annigan. He waved his long fingers through the air; they left a shimmering trail of light behind. 'You see, I know everything there is to know about dragons, sure and that's a fact.'

Questrid exchanged an excited look with Copper.

Mr Annigan went on, 'The dragons called me. It's as simple as that. When they have a problem, Shane Annigan's the man!'

Everyone stared at him.

'Are the dragons like our dragons – friendly, I mean?' asked Copper.

'Ruby has a little dragon called Glinty,' Questrid told him. 'She's friendly.'

'Your mother has one? Does she now? Dragons are most mysterious,' went on Mr Annigan. 'They are an ancient race, the dragons . . . ' His voice dipped to a whisper. 'Oh, there's many a story about the dragon world.'

And then, without anyone quite knowing how, he began to tell them stories of fantastic dragons, dangerous dragons, dragons that could cast spells and dragons with fish tails that could swim and breathe underwater. Everyone, even Amy much against her wishes, was spellbound. When he stopped they were still as statues, leaning forward and waiting for more.

'We've been so impolite,' said Amber, getting up quickly. 'We've done nothing, only let you entertain us!'

'Well, now,' said Mr Annigan, 'that's fine. But I'd be most grateful if you'd let me stay the night here, then I'll set off tomorrow and be at Dragon Mountain as quickly as I can.'

'Of course,' said Cedar. 'Come with me. I'll show you where you can sleep.'

'That man'd be useful if you were lost in a dark night, wouldn't he?' said Uncle Greenwood. 'Now he's gone I can hardly see.'

The room had dulled when Shane Annigan left. Questrid shivered. 'Seems cold now,' he said.

Amy played with the ends of her long hair nervously. She didn't like Shane Annigan. He'd said something strange, what was it? Something wrong... She tapped her finger against the table. She watched Copper stroking the cub's head. The cub was butting her gently under the chin.

Don't love it so much, Copper. I wish you wouldn't, thought Amy. Please don't. Nobody should love a little old wolf cub the way you do, silly girl. Silly Wood girl.

'I'm just taking Ralick out.' Copper dragged on a heavy coat and headed for the door.

'Me too,' said Questrid.

Amy waited for them to ask her as well, but they didn't. It was as though they had completely forgotten

74

her existence. She watched Questrid pulling a woolly hat down over Copper's hair so it covered her eyes. She watched Copper flick him with the end of her scarf so he laughed. It all hurt. Jealousy. It was a new sensation, one she barely recognised, only feeling it like a punch in the stomach.

They hadn't invited her. They didn't want her. Questrid didn't like her.

I don't care, she told herself. Leave me out, ignore me. I don't care because I've got Granite. Ow! Hollow words. I don't want Granite! I want Copper and Questrid! I want to stay here! I want them to like me.

She got up. She knew what she had to do: tell them everything. Amy slipped outside.

The wind had died down. It was quiet and still. Snow lay heaped around Spindle House in high sculptured banks, whipped into magical shapes like giant meringues. The night was crisp and clear, millions of stars glinting in the sky.

Amy stopped beneath the cover of the porch, alerted by a gruff, low voice. Nobody had seen her.

'Wish I was lit up like a lantern,' said the new voice from deep in the shadows by the stables. 'Can't see a thing.'

Amy felt a shiver up her spine; it was the voice from Copper's room last night. Who could it be?

Questrid laughed. 'It would be great, wouldn't it? Isn't Shane fantastic? Oh, I'd love to be a dragon expert like him. I want to travel and have adventures too.'

'I loved his stories, but don't you think he's just a bit creepy?' asked Copper. 'His eyes are a bit flat and—'

'No! I just thought he was great. What do you think, Ralick?'

'My highly-tuned wolverine senses are suspicious of anyone arriving by such "chance",' said the gruff, small voice. 'I may only have the brain of a cuddly wolf cub, but I thought he was too bright and too sharp.'

'Oh, Ralick!' Questrid laughed.

Ralick! Ralick! It was the little wolf cub speaking! Amy bit back a cry of surprise. The wolf could talk!

No wonder Granite wanted him, thought Amy. How much more valuable was a talking wolf cub than an ordinary one. Why hadn't Granite told her? Why hadn't *they* told her? Why hadn't anyone shared this secret with her?

Because nobody likes you, she told herself. Nobody really likes or trusts you. You're a spoiler. A horrible, sad little spoiler.

Amy slipped quickly back into the kitchen. Everyone was busy cooking or talking. They didn't notice her. Her heart was heavy as lead. She could barely move. She slumped in her chair. I can't steal the cub, he'll yell when I grab him. It's impossible. Granite will be so angry... I'll have to go back to Aunt Agnes and Uncle John...

Copper and Questrid came back. They began to lay the long kitchen table for supper. Amy willed herself to get up. She felt as though she had a boulder strapped to her back. She had to smile. Had to pretend she was all right.

76

Copper was whispering to her soup spoon.

'You're the only person I've ever met who talks to cutlery,' Amy said as cheerily as she could.

'It won't behave,' Copper said. 'It's almost as bad as that one we gave you. It's sycamore wood and it spins around like a whirligig and tips out my soup. It's a joker.'

'A balsa wood spoon for Mr Shane Annigan, I think,' said Questrid. He put the lightest spoon they had beside his bowl. 'He doesn't look like he could hold anything heavier... Hey, wouldn't you love to go to Dragon Mountain?' he added. He slid an extra chair to the table. 'Doesn't it sound fantastic? I'd love my own dragon. Can you imagine how cool that would be? Not one like Glinty, she just sits on her bed of gold and snores.'

'You'd better not let Aunt Ruby hear you talking like that about her dear Glinty,' said Copper.

'Just as well she's not here tonight,' said Questrid.

'I wish she was, though,' said Copper. 'I miss her so much.'

'You know my mum better than me,' said Questrid. 'But even I know she loves living in the Rock.'

'I don't understand,' said Amy. 'How can Copper know her better than you?'

'Well, I've only got to know her again recently,' Questrid said. 'Ruby lost me when I was six. She went South. She brought Copper up there. Ruby thought Copper was an orphan, you see.'

Shane Annigan came in. Questrid pretended to be blinded. He staggered back with his hands over his eyes. 'Don't you keep yourself awake at night?'

Shane laughed. 'No, no. I've these smart photo-receptors in my skin which react, you see, to the amount of light around me. So, when it's the darkness that's coming on, I'm light. But I can think myself darker too. Watch me, then.'

He closed his eyes, set his fingertips together and breathed deeply. His shimmering light faded to a gentle warm glow. He opened his eyes. 'See?'

'Brilliant!' said Questrid.

'Do sit down, Mr Annigan,' said Amber. She carried some dishes to the table.

'I *am* very hungry,' Mr Annigan said. 'I travelled all the long day and then getting lost in the snow...'

'Like you, Questrid,' said Copper.

'I see that wolf cub never leaves you, does he, Copper?' Shane said.

'No, we're always together. He's called Ralick after a special toy I had,' she told him. 'I've still got the first Ralick, but, well, I'm too old for toys. He took over where Ralick left off and so he's named Ralick too.'

'He looks like very intelligent; I can see it in his eyes, whereas with dragons—'

'What?' Questrid asked.

'There's two things to consider with dragons. One, the smoke. If the smoke comes out of the left nostril, the dragon is very clever, from the right nostril, not so clever.'

'And what else?'

'A clever dragon is so clever it will direct its smoke out the wrong way, just to confuse you, you see, and make you think it's stupid.'

'But, but that means you never know whether a dragon's clever or not!' said Copper.

'Exactly so! Tricky things, dragons. But your cub – he's got an aura – makes him special.'

'I think Mr Annigan's teasing you, dear,' said Amber, gently.

'Oh, not really, Mrs Beech. My what delicious food this is. What a kind family. Why, d'you know, this is quite the cosiest house I've ever been in.' He leaned back in his chair and folded his arms over his chest.

'It is,' agreed Copper. 'It's alive. You will hear the way it creaks and whispers. You can't do anything you shouldn't here – if you do, the place makes such a racket!'

'Interesting.' Mr Annigan laughed lightly. 'If I'm to get up to a spot of mischief, it had better be out of doors I'm thinking!'

13
Can She, Can't She?

In the morning they saw how the snowstorm had
changed the landscape. Snow had hidden rocks, bushes
and trees beneath a thick white blanket. Half the house
was enclosed behind a gigantic snowdrift. Everything
looked fresh and clean.

'It's lucky that Mr Annigan is so light-footed,' said
Amber. She put porridge into the breakfast bowls. 'If he
was heavy he'd sink into these great snowdrifts and
never be seen again!'

'Ah, you are so right,' said Shane Annigan, coming in
at that moment. 'I am as light as a mite of dust and will
float over the crystals like a flake of snow myself. Is that
porridge? Lovely. Do you know,' he added, 'that snow
fairies freeze porridge and use it as missiles? I once had
a fight with a giant yeti, sure, he was a brute of a
creature, living up on a lonely mountain top. I flew
round and round him, riding my dragon like a warplane,

bombarding him with frozen fairy porridge balls.'

'Cool!' breathed Questrid. 'Oh, I wish I could!'

'Questrid, don't worry. It'll all be there for you when the time is right,' said Greenwood.

'Well, I've had a lovely time here, and that's the truth,' said Shane. 'But now, before I go, might I have a look at the Root Room you've told me about?'

The Root Room was where Greenwood, Cedar and Amber worked at wood carving. It was a big, natural room made beneath the fanned out roots of the spindle tree.

Amy and Copper followed Cedar and Shane down the narrow stairs. The strong, sweet smell of the wood and fresh wood shavings made Amy cough and her eyes water.

'We're making a mirror at the moment,' Cedar said. 'We have a buyer in the South. Someone who appreciates our work.'

The mirror stood two metres high. It was made from walnut and rosewood, and carved with animals and flowers. One side of the frame was patterned with filigree strands of gold and embedded with silver and precious stones, the other side was still to be decorated.

'That's mighty fine,' said Shane. 'Those strands of gold are so delicate.'

'My wife does those intricate bits,' said Cedar proudly.

'And you've got plenty of gold, have you?' asked Shane Annigan.

Cedar went so still that Amy knew he was shocked. Or angry. Something about Shane's question disturbed

81

him. Did he wonder if Shane had heard the stories of Amber knitting gold too? Maybe he had? Maybe he was hoping to get some himself.

'We're trading with the Rockers again, now,' Cedar said. 'There's plenty of gold coming out of the mountains.'

'Do you enjoy making things, Amethyst?' Shane asked. Amy shrugged. In her mind's eye she saw the hunched forms of the grey clay gargoyles on the stone table at home. 'I'm quite good at some things,' she said. 'But I—'

'Yes?'

'But, well, I've never tried to make anything *beautiful*.'

'So what have you made? Just ugly things?' Copper laughed.

It was on the tip of Amy's tongue to say 'yes'. How wonderful if she could fling herself into Amber's arms and confess all. If only Shane Annigan wasn't glaring at her with his cold, light eyes. Amy went red. She shook her head. 'I've made nothing.'

They watched Amber's long, nimble fingers wind the gold thread through minuscule holes in the wooden mirror frame. She bent it and plaited it and knotted it into flowers, birds and stars. Watching her made Amy's insides shrink and tangle. How could anyone do such delicate, clever things? How did the birds and the flowers look so real? She studied Amber; it wasn't hard to imagine her making gold.

'See this flower here, Amethyst?' Amber pointed to a blue stone with a darker centre. 'That's a Star

Amethyst. It's a very special stone, an amethyst with a flaw in its centre. The flaw makes it more valuable. They're rare.'

'Oh,' said Amy.

A vast wave of sadness washed over her, so violent was it, that she nearly fell over. I'm a spoiled amethyst, she thought. There's no hope for me. Flawed. Ruined. She bit her bottom lip to stop it from trembling. She didn't even hear the last words Amber had said about the Star Amethyst being the most valuable and rare.

Cedar was carving a rosebud from a knob of brown wood and they watched as it grew like a watered seed bursting into life before their eyes.

'It's truly wonderful, so it is,' Shane said.

'I wish I could do it,' said Copper.

'You'll soon learn,' said Amber.

'You must spend more time learning the techniques, Copper,' said Shane Annigan. 'Making anything fine takes time. Will you work really hard this afternoon, just for me?'

'Oh, all right. I'll try.'

'After all, she must be able to do it; it's in her blood,' said Cedar.

'Maybe it isn't,' said Copper. 'I can knit. Only I don't any more,' she added, glancing at her mother. She exchanged a look with Amy. There'd be no knitting without knitting needles, her look said.

At last Shane Annigan was ready to continue his journey. They accompanied him to the front door.

'That's a fine species of dragon you have there,'

Shane said. He was looking up at the dragon carved out of the lintel above the door.

'A Marble Mountain Dragon,' said Cedar. 'A good luck charm.'

'Splendid! I hope you always have good fortune. Goodbye to you all and many thanks!' Shane stepped out across the snow, waving merrily to them.

He started off walking lightly on the white crust, his feet hardly marking its surface. Suddenly he broke into a run. His clothes flapped loosely round him. The faster he went, the higher off the ground he seemed to go, until he was almost flying and running at the same time. His white clothes seemed to mingle with the white of the snow until finally he became a blur and vanished into the distance.

'Wow!' said Copper. 'Fantastic!'

'I'm going to all those places he told us about one day,' said Questrid. 'You see if I don't.'

'Well, I'm not,' said Copper. 'I love it here. I'm never going. Amy, come down to the Root Room with me, will you? I promised Mr Annigan I'd work harder – though I'm really hopeless. Questrid's got some lumps of stone down there that you could carve. We could be together.'

So they both went down to the Root Room.

'Amy, would you like to try marble, granite, or basalt?' said Cedar.

'Marble,' said Amy, without hesitating. Marble was cold and hard to work with. If there were faults in the stone, and there always were, it might chip and could

84

shatter. But that made it all the more challenging. The end results were smooth and sophisticated.

'OK. Copper has an elm figure,' said Cedar. 'She's only been working on it for three months, Amy,' he joked, 'that's why it's so good.'

Copper held up the piece of knobbly elm. It didn't look like anything.

'Hopeless!' she said. 'Let's see who can produce the worst piece by the end of the afternoon!'

Amy looked up at the domed tangle of roots above their heads. How would she bear it down here? The roots cascaded down the sides, then disappeared into the earth walls. Built into the spaces between the roots were small cupboards, shelves and racks for hanging the tools on. Compared to the white walls, smooth floors of shiny rock and snow-reflected light which she'd had in Granite's studio, she did not find it very inspiring.

She had to make do with Questrid's spare tools, because the ones Uncle John had given her were back at Malachite Mountain. She stroked the chunk of marble. She turned it round and round. For the very first time she was going to carve something beautiful. She began to chisel and chip at the stone. She forgot everything else.

Alongside her, Copper worked on her wooden figure.

'Wood's so difficult,' she whispered to Amy. 'Not like knitting. I can knit every stitch there is, you know, and quickly, too.'

'Not much good if your mum won't let you,' said Amy.

Copper shrugged. 'Wish I knew why.'

For two hours Copper and Amy worked, chatting all the time. They gouged and cut, sanded and polished. Finally Copper threw down her figure in disgust.

'It's horrible! Look! I've just sliced off her nose and she looks like a pig. I can't do it, Cedar, I can't!'

'Er, I'm not sure your mother is right about your carving talents being *hidden*.' He studied the figure. 'More like non-existent. What about you, Amy?'

'I haven't got very far,' said Amy. She blew the dust off her sculpture and handed it to Cedar.

Copper grabbed it before Cedar could take it.

'Oh, Amy, this is fantastic! It's me, isn't it? It's brilliant!'

Amy hadn't had any intention of sculpting Copper's head, but every time she'd looked up, that had been what she saw. Even though it was nowhere near finished, it did have something of Copper about it.

'It is lovely, Amy. You're very talented,' said Cedar.

'Oh, Amy, it's great! Can I have it when it's done?'

''Course you can.'

'Thanks.'

Copper snatched off her apron, dusted the wood shavings from her clothes and gave her a hug. 'Let's get out of here!'

Amy stood for a moment. The feel of Copper's hands pressed against her back, still there, as if indentations had been left in soft clay. Even the Woody smell of her lingered. It should have been disgusting, repulsive even. But it wasn't. It was a good feeling. Amy had never been hugged since her mother died. She didn't know what she'd been missing. Her eyes were misty. She stumbled up the stairs.

'Sometimes, I really wonder if I have any Wood blood in me,' Copper said. 'I'm so bad at so many Woody things. Mmm, smell that cake!' She made a funny face, lifting her eyebrows and licking her lips. 'Maybe I got more Rock blood from Amber's side than Wood from Dad's. I'm glad Questrid is half-Rock and half-Wood too. Nice to share our insides like that. Oh, sorry, Amy. I mean there's nothing wrong with being *entirely* Rock. You are and you're very nice.'

Oriole was sitting in the kitchen, reading *The Secret Life of a Blackbird*. Lots of small birds hopped about in her lap, pecking at a pile of seeds.

'That cake smells great! Where's Questrid?' Copper asked. 'He's usually around when a cake's been made. Where's Ralick?'

'Ralick? Isn't he with you?' said Oriole.

'No. I've been in the Root Room. He waits in the kitchen usually. In his basket. I never thought...I was so busy...That's odd!' Copper went very still. The pink faded from her cheeks.

Amy pressed her hands over her stomach. Something which usually held it up, seemed to have let it go. She gulped. Poor Copper. Then, almost immediately, she corrected herself. *Poor Copper?* Never mind Copper, she told herself. You should have been watching out for that cub. Why weren't you thinking about him? You've got so distracted by this

87

Wood family, you've forgotten what you're doing here! Aunt Agnes's unwelcome voice popped into her head: '*Spoiler! You've spoiled your chance! You'd spoil anything, you would!*'

'Something's wrong,' said Copper. She chewed her lower lip. 'Ralick never goes anywhere.'

'Well, he hasn't truly disappeared yet,' said Amy. 'May-be he's locked in your room? Or in the stables? The garden?'

Copper was out of the room in a flash. She bounded up the spiral staircase to the upper floors. Amy checked all the rooms on the ground floor. Upstairs she heard Copper racing along the corridors, slamming the doors, shouting for Ralick.

'Nothing!' Copper called. She careered down the stairs. 'I feel so bad. I've got this feeling. Oh, Amy . . . He's gone!'

They hurried across the kitchen. Copper picked up her old Ralick, a moth-eaten cuddly toy and hugged him. She kissed his black thread nose.

'Ralick, Ralick,' she whispered. 'Where are you?'

'No sign of him?' asked Oriole.

'Nothing.'

Copper was already at the back door pulling on warmer clothes. Amy followed her, dragging on water-proof boots.

They ran out to the stables. Thunder and Lightning greeted Copper by tossing their great heads and pawing the ground. Copper patted them quickly then raced up the wooden steps to Questrid's bedroom.

'Questrid! Questrid! Ralick!' she called. She flung

open the door. But the room was empty. 'I knew it!' she sobbed. 'I knew they weren't there!'

She spun round, nearly knocking Amy over and scooted back down the steps. She ran out into the garden and over the snow-covered lawns, calling all the time.

Amy ran after her. Someone's taken him. I was supposed to do it! Oh, what will Granite say? What'll happen now?

They ran all over the garden but there was no sign of either Questrid or Ralick.

'Where could they be?' Copper said. 'Sometimes Questrid goes up to the Rock, but he never takes Ralick. What d'you think, Amy?'

'I don't know. I'm sure he's OK, Copper. He's probably asleep somewhere, all curled up and—'

'No, no! I know he isn't!' Copper's eyes shone.

The sun came out from behind the high thin cloud for a few minutes and bathed the garden in a weak, lemony yellow haze. Far up on the ridge behind Spindle House, a quick movement caught Amy's eye.

She stared, shielding her eyes from the dazzle, but whatever had moved had gone now. She thought of Shane Annigan and the sense of foreboding hanging over her deepened.

'Ralick, Ralick, Ralick,' Copper chanted. As if that would make him appear. 'Amy! I need him!'

'I know,' Amy said, although she didn't. Not really. She'd never cared for anything.

'If Ralick has gone with Questrid they'll have left tracks,' she said. 'We must go and look.'

They trudged through the deep snow back to the front door. They examined the snow.

'Those light marks and shallow indentations are Shane Annigan's,' said Amy. 'But look there.'

She pointed at some deeper footsteps.

'I recognise the pattern of the sole. Those were new boots,' Copper said, softly. '*Questrid's* boots! But he wouldn't take Ralick!'

Copper began to run alongside the track of marks. Amy went too. They stopped when they reached the end of the garden where the great wooden wall marked the beginning of the outside. Questrid's footsteps carried on through the gate, shadowing Shane's footsteps. Disappearing into the distance.

'Remember how he was talking about going adventuring?' said Amy. 'Shane Annigan so inspired him with all that dragon talk, maybe he . . . '

Copper stared into the distance. She put her hands up to her throat as if something was stuck there, choking her. Her eyes swam with tears.

'Took Ralick?' she whispered. 'Without telling me?'

'I don't know,' said Amy. 'Maybe they'll both be inside when we go in. It will all be all right.'

But it wasn't.

Ralick and Questrid had both disappeared.

14
Questrid the Hunter

While Copper and Amy had worked in the Root Room, Questrid had been in his room above the stable. Daydreaming. He was imagining himself speeding through the air on a sleek silver dragon. He was circling a dark and mysterious castle. Around him, evil brown dragons with red tongues and blazing red eyes gathered for the kill...

Then something broke into his dreams and he sat up. He went to the window and looked out into the yard. A glimmer of light, mirrored and reflected on the snow, caught his attention. Shane Annigan!

'What's he doing back?' And just for a second, Questrid's soul soared, thinking maybe he'd come back for him. Maybe he wanted Questrid to be his travelling companion. Questrid was about to rap his fingers on the glass to catch Shane's attention, when he heard a squeal.
Ralick!

91

Then he saw the cub. It was like a punch in the stomach. He gasped. Shane Annigan *had* Ralick. He was stuffing the struggling, yelping cub into a white sack!

'He's *stealing* Ralick!'

Questrid ran to the door – it was locked. Impossible! He tugged and pulled at the handle. How could it be locked? There wasn't even a keyhole! He dashed back to the window but it was too small for him to get through. Anyway he knew he'd then be stuck on the roof. Shane Annigan was moving fast. He was already on the other side of the great wall. If I don't do something straight away, he thought, I'll never catch him.

He raced back to the door.

Look, he told himself, calmly, it cannot be locked because there is no key. There must be something holding it. Think logically.

He twisted the handle again. Something was stopping it from turning. There were some silvery wisps of thread there. *Cobwebs?* Weird! The internal workings of the doorknob were tangled up with cobweb.

Questrid dragged his box of tools out from beneath his bed. He opened it and rummaged around for a screwdriver. Instead he found one of Copper's old crochet hooks. He slipped it into his pocket, thinking how glad she'd be to see that again.

He found a screwdriver of the right size and began to unscrew the door handle. He was so frantic, his fingers slipped and slithered and he gouged great chunks from the door.

'Come on!' he yelled. 'Come on, you clumsy oaf!'

Finally the handle was off. Questrid goggled. It was as if a crazy spider had sneaked into the door. It seemed to have spun, tangled, twisted and knotted miles of fine, gossamer-like threads into a dense mass.

Questrid shook his head in amazement. 'That's just weird.'

He attacked the thread with his chisel. His screwdriver. Everything. But the stuff was stronger than wire. He couldn't undo it. He'd have to dismantle it. It took him ages to undo the inside part of the catch. At last he did. He pulled out the thread. It was woven like a dormouse nest.

Questrid quickly refitted the handle and opened the door. He was free!

He pulled on his coat and scarf and ran.

Down the stairs, into the garden. Down to the gates. Out into the wide-open snowy plain. The ruffled snow showed exactly the way Shane Annigan had gone.

With Ralick.

Questrid walked for a long time. The only living thing he saw on his journey was Glinty, Ruby's dragon. She circled and swooped high in the sky, a blur of turquoise flashes and sparks above the Rock. Apart from that, the white landscape was empty and entirely still.

15
Missing

'I can't bear it, I can't bear it without my Ralick,'
Copper sobbed. She threw herself onto her bed. 'Where
is he?'

Amy stared at her, suddenly scornful. Weak and sappy
thing, she thought. She remembered the tabby kitten
she'd wanted. Aunt Agnes had drowned it. *You see big
eyes and fluff, that's what you see, but it's fleas and filth
that I see. And pulling on your heart strings. No. No!*

And so Amy's heart strings had remained unpulled.

Now she was determined to fulfil her contract with
Granite. She would do it, despite Copper. At least
Granite was powerful and stony. No weeping there and
neither did Amy weep.

'I wasn't going to say anything,' said Amy, sitting
down beside Copper. 'But now...'

'What?'

'It's just that I think Questrid took Ralick,' said Amy.

94

'He was jealous of the way we were getting on. He felt pushed out... I think he wished I'd never come here.'

Copper sat up and grabbed her arm. 'But Questrid's so, so...' She paused. 'Well, so good! I can't believe it.'

'What else can explain Ralick's disappearance?'

'I don't know...'

'Questrid looks at me so strangely. Tries to avoid me,' went on Amy. 'He's never liked me. Shane inspired him and now I bet he's gone off to look for dragons. With Ralick.'

'No! He wouldn't... He loves Ralick, I know, but he wouldn't steal him and Ralick would never go without me!'

'Ah, yes, you're probably right,' said Amy, quietly. 'It's mean of me—'

'No, sorry! You *could* be right...' said Copper. 'I'll tell Cedar. And Mum. They'll know what to do. I HAVE to get Ralick back!'

'Why don't we go and look?' said Amy.

She moved to the window and stared out at the sun twinkling on the snow. *I've* got to get that wolf cub back, she thought. The sooner we set out, the better the chance we have of finding him. 'We could just follow the footsteps a little way. If we leave it too long, they'll disappear...'

'D'you think so?'

'Grown-ups will only try and stop us...' said Amy.

They crept back downstairs again. The wooden staircase groaned and squeaked and creaked and whined.

'Shh! Shh!' Copper said.

Amy knew the wood wanted Copper to stay.

The kitchen, unusually, was empty.

'Let's take some cake,' said Amy. She scooped up a couple of slices from the plate. 'And drink.' She stuffed a bottle of water and the cake into Copper's backpack, which was by the door.

'But we'll only be a few minutes...'

'Just in case,' said Amy. She had a feeling they might be away some time.

'I ought to tell someone what we're doing,' whispered Copper. 'It's not right...'

'Don't worry.'

'I suppose we'll come back as soon as we've seen which way they went... And maybe Questrid's hurt? Or Ralick? Perhaps there's been an accident? I'm so lucky I've got you, Amethyst.'

Amy felt sick to the pit of her stomach at her duplicity.

But still I'll go on, she thought. Yes, I'll go on and spoil it all for Copper, because that's what I came for. That's my job. Spoiler. Wrecker. And it won't really matter in the end, when I'm rich. Granite will be pleased. I bet he makes me his heir. The new Lord, no, *Queen* of the Rock People...

They reached the gateway. Swathes of whiteness spread out all around them. The mountain peaks seemed suddenly closer. The wooded slopes looked dark and menacing. It was different here. Already Amy could feel what it meant to be away from Spindle House. The influence of the Wood Clan was waning.

'It's so lonely out here,' Copper whispered, hugging herself.

'It'll be all right. We're together.'

'You're so brave, Amy. You Rock people are stronger than us Woods in so many ways. Mum and Dad will be worried...'

My aunt and uncle let me go easily enough, thought Amy. Nobody hurt or worried there. So why should I care?

Shane Annigan's light footsteps left almost no mark. His cape brushed the ground and left a soft sweeping line over the snow, like a big snail trail. This was the mark that Questrid had followed earlier.

They went up the side of the hill, following Questrid's tracks, through the woods, towards the distant purple mountains. When they got to the top of the first hill, they turned and looked back at Spindle House.

'Oh, Amy!' said Copper. 'Isn't it the most wonderful house in the world? I wish I'd left a note. I hope they're not worried.'

'They won't even have noticed we've gone,' said Amy.

They walked for an hour and there was still no sight of Ralick or Questrid.

'Maybe we should go back now,' said Copper.

'Well, we could if you really wanted to,' said Amy. 'But I think there's some sort of cave or tunnel up there. Shall we go and see?'

I am not going back without that wolf cub, Amy told herself. And if Questrid brought him this way, I have to go this way too.

They reached the tunnel. Amy wondered if this was the one-way tunnel that Granite had told her about. She felt sure it was.

Go through alone, or with Copper? *With* Copper, she decided quickly. It was better being with someone. Not so scary. And if Ralick was on the other side, he'd want to come to Copper. He might not come to Amy. Yes, she definitely needed Copper with her.

Copper was examining the snow beside the tunnel. 'Questrid's footprints are everywhere!' she said.

'Well, at least we know we're on the right path,' said Amy. 'Questrid must be carrying Ralick.'

Amy noticed another set of prints. They were fresh. They were Shane Annigan's, she was sure.

Amy was shocked but not surprised.

She remembered with a jolt something Shane had said in the kitchen. Questrid had mentioned Ruby, and Shane Annigan had known she was Questrid's mother. *How* did he know that? How did he know *anything* about Ruby if he'd just been blown to Spindle House like he said?

I never trusted him. Amy clenched her fists. I was right.

She wiped away the marks before Copper could see them. Shane must have the wolf cub, then, she thought. And Questrid went after *him*. I might have known it.

'Do you think they've gone in?' asked Copper. She was leaning into the tunnel. 'It's so cold and dark in there. It gives me the creeps! The air's all musty and dank, like an old black blanket,' she said. 'It's horrid. I've got goose bumps. My neck's gone all prickly. Amy, I'm scared! I'm sure we shouldn't go in.'

Amy didn't fancy going through the tunnel either. She tried to remember exactly what Granite had told her about it. Something about Wood People not being able to use it? What exactly did one-way mean?

While they were wondering what to do, Amy heard a noise on the mountain below them. Someone was coming.

'We'll be fine together,' said Amy, grabbing Copper's arm. 'Come on. In we go.'

A loud noise stopped them. A big white bird was circling above them. 'Kwaar! Kwaar!' it called. It flew down and landed on a rock beside the tunnel mouth.

'Casimir!' said Copper. 'Maybe he's got a message.'

She knelt beside the bird and opened the message tube tied to its leg. She pulled a tiny roll of paper out, but it was blank. 'Nothing . . .'

Casimir made a cross screeching sound. He bobbed his head up and down and bounced fretfully on his orange legs. 'Kwaar!' His big feet left triangular prints in the snow as he marched around. 'Kwaar!'

'I think he doesn't want us to go in,' said Copper. 'If he says no then—'

'He's just an old bird,' said Amy, thinking quickly. 'He probably came so you could send a message home, that's all.'

'Do you think so? OK. I'll leave a message then.' Copper took a pencil from her backpack and wrote a note.

Don't worry. We're going after Q and R through the tunnel. Back soon.

C xxx

Copper fitted the roll of paper back in the holder on the bird's stick-like leg.

'Let's go,' said Amy. She made a face at Casimir. Hah, nearly stopped us, she told it silently. Only I'm too clever! Good try, birdie!

Casimir rose into the air. He glided off through the fir trees, crying miserably.

Amy was sure she heard a scrabbling noise further down the hill. Someone else was following them. She urged Copper into the tunnel.

The atmosphere inside the rock was entirely different from the outside. The air was thick, damp and very cold. To move even one step forward, Amy saw that Copper had to lean against the air, pushing with all her weight. After a few steps she coughed and gasped for breath.

'I think this is wrong. We shouldn't—'

'I don't expect it's far,' said Amy. She sucked the icy air in. She pushed against the invisible force. 'Come on, it's not that bad. Think about Ralick.'

She dragged Copper on.

There was a dim blue light in the tunnel. It came from the glowing, blue ice wall. It reminded Amy of the light in the butcher's shop back home. The air felt too empty and scentless for anything to survive in it.

As they went further, the tunnel walls closed in on them. The roof grew lower. It got harder and harder to walk.

'I can't do it,' Copper whispered. She clutched at Amy. 'Amy, I'll have to go back. I'm not as strong as you. I know I'm half-Rock, but . . . This is your element, it's OK for you, it's agony for me.' She stumbled. 'Please, Amy, please.'

'No. You can't go back,' said Amy. Someone was coming through the tunnel behind them, she was sure. 'Think of Ralick. Think of your Rock soul. Rock blood. We have to—'

They had made their way round a small bend in the tunnel. A circle of brighter white light appeared ahead.

'Look, look! The end's in sight!' She had to force herself not to add, Quickly! Quickly! Come on you feeble, bendy wooden thing!

Again Amy heard a sound. Footsteps were padding over the icy path towards them. Not heavy. Not very fast, but purposeful. She glanced behind. A figure was approaching. Running towards them, arms waving.

Copper was too preoccupied with just breathing to notice.

But Amy thought she recognised the figure . . . 'Run!' she yelled. 'Quick!'

Copper didn't even look back. She lunged forward, half-dragged by Amy. She skidded and slipped.

Just ten strides brought them to the end of the corridor. They burst out into the open.

'Who was it?' whispered Copper. She was trembling all over. Her cheeks were pale. Amy was scared she might collapse.

They stared back at the person now standing at the bend in the narrow tunnel.

Amy sank down in the snow as if she were exhausted. 'I don't know.'

Copper let out a little cry of anguish. 'Oh, Amy, I think it's . . .'

16
On the Other Side of the Mountain

'It's *Cedar*!' cried Copper.

'Is it?' Amy pretended to be surprised.

'Yes. See! Thank goodness... Why's he stopped?'

Cedar was waving his arms. He hammered his fist in front of his face, as if banging a solid wall. He was shouting – but they couldn't hear a sound.

'I'm coming!' Copper ran back into the tunnel. Two paces in, she smacked against an invisible wall and was flung back into the snow.

The tunnel was blocked.

Now Amy understood what Granite had meant. There was no going back.

'Cedar! Dad!' sobbed Copper. 'I want him. All I want is my dad!'

'Of course,' said Amy, coldly. 'You've got a dad. I've no one. No one ever wants me.' Now you know what it's like, she added silently.

'Amy! I never thought.' Copper spun round. 'I am sorry. I'm so selfish!'

Oh, blast you! I can't even be horrid to you! Amy was speechless. Are you coated with glass or something? she thought. No matter how many horrid remarks I make, no matter how mean I am, it all bounces off without a scratch.

'I felt it right at the start,' said Copper. 'There was something wrong with that tunnel. I could tell it was spooky and weird, but I pretended it wasn't. I'm so stupid. I was so keen to find Ralick... now we've no choice. We'll have to go on.'

Cedar and Copper stared at each other down the blue of the tunnel.

'I'm going to find Ralick!' Copper called. She pointed away from the tunnel, trying to tell him she was going on. 'SORRY!' she shouted. 'SORRY!'

She turned away. 'This is so awful.' She turned to Amy. 'What shall we do?'

'Cedar won't go till you do, Copper,' Amy said.

Copper nodded. 'You're right.'

She turned and walked away.

It was like coming to a new world. Snow-covered peaks, which hadn't been visible on the other side, spiked the air, like giant teeth. Green-tinged clouds circled their summits. Miles and miles below, a wide river meandered through a deep snowless gorge where vast forests of tall, broad-leaved trees edged the river. Small snow-covered hills dipped and rose around them for as far as the eye could see.

'I smell smoke,' said Amy.

The smoke streamed from the chimneys of a cluster of small, pale-coloured houses. The buildings were sheltering against a rocky outcrop not far away. A path cut into the deep snow led towards the houses.

'Let's go down there. They might have seen Questrid and Ralick,' said Amy.

The light was beginning to fade. They tramped silently down the hill.

'Those houses are odd,' said Amy. 'We're getting nearer, but have you noticed, they aren't getting any bigger?'

The houses were miniature houses. They were made entirely out of ice, but they were not igloo-shaped, they were house-shaped. They had ice chimneys and ice-tiled roofs. Some had towers and pinnacles, even gables over the little diamond-shaped windows. Around each house, a low ice wall surrounded an ice garden full of ice sculptures. There were ice rose bushes, trees, birds and animals. There were also peculiar constructions which Amy thought must be wind chimes because as they got nearer, she heard them tinkling tunefully in the wind.

They were about to go through the ice gate of the first house, when the front door opened and a tiny person rushed out. He wasn't much taller than a four-year- old human child. He was dressed in a jerkin, blue tights and pointed boots. He had white skin, a pointed nose and pointed ears. He had a bit of white beard on the tip of his chin.

'Hello,' Copper said. 'We're looking for—'

'Go away! We don't want your sort here! Go on! Leg it!'

Copper and Amy looked at each other in amazement, then back down at the little person whose pale grey eyes were scrunched up with anger. His yellow-white hair flew out around his head like a dandelion clock.

'Excuse me?' Copper said.

'You heard me! Get out of here. *Aliens!*' He waved his tiny fist at them and curled up his pale mouth in a snarl. 'Go back to the other side, go on! Dragon Destroyers!'

'But—'

Then the ice house door was snatched open again, and a second, younger-looking, tiny pale person bolted out. He caught hold of the first little person by his arm and hissed at him.

'Hush, hush, Grampy. They're not aliens. Come along in now.' He grinned sheepishly at Copper and Amy. 'Sorry.' He led the angry little character back inside. He shut the door on him, then rushed back to the gate. 'So sorry,' he said, breathlessly. 'Delightedly-thrilled to meet you. I'm Squitcher.'

Amy shook his hand – it was like shaking the fragile, tiny paw of a mouse.

'That was my Grampy,' he said. '*Grumpy* we call him. Did you come through the tunnel? Are you from the Other Side?'

They nodded.

'Jolly, jolly,' said Squitcher. 'Grampy's upset. It's Boldly Seer, our dragon, you know. Grampy's sure we've had a Dragon Destroyer. What are you then, strange pair?' He jumped onto the wall and peered into their faces. 'Well, well!' He gathered a handful of Copper's red-gold hair and slithered it through his fingers. 'Not Rock! Not Wood! Not Air! Not Ice! Not even Water!'

'I'm Wood *and* Stone,' said Copper. 'And Amy is—'

'Let me guess. Let me guess!' Squitcher screeched with delight. He pulled a long dark strand of hair out from under Amy's woolly hat and sniffed it. 'Rock. Through and through. Hard as hard.'

'Thanks,' said Amy. She tried to smile. 'What are you, anyway?'

'We're pixicles!'

'*Pixicles?*'

'We're icy cold pixies!' said Squitcher. 'We're jolly, jolly chilly-cold all the time but we don't mind. What are you doing here?'

'Looking for someone,' said Copper.

'A boy and a wolf cub,' said Amy. 'The boy stole the wolf cub and we're trying to get it back.'

'Amy, we don't know that for sure,' said Copper.

'Whatever,' said Amy. She stared up at the sky.

'Ah ha,' said Squitcher, mysteriously. 'We found something today, it's some sort of a boy. Come and see. Things are weird today. Grampy says a Dragon Destroyer passed by... Getting dark,' observed Squitcher. He jumped down from the wall. 'Follow me.'

It was twilight. The sky had darkened to the deepest lavender blue and stars twinkled. Copper looked wistful. Amy guessed she was thinking of Spindle House and of

106

sitting by the fire with Ralick. Amy thought of her own chamber in Malachite Mountain, of ordering a rock-goyle to straighten out her bed sheets and bring her a large glass of mint tea...Where would they spend the night tonight?

As darkness fell, the lights in the ice houses were turned on. They glowed and shone through the ice walls. Amy could see more pixicles inside the houses. It was a bit like looking inside compartments in a freezer.

Squitcher led them past lots of houses. There were tiny white faces watching them at many of the windows. Behind the houses there was a vast cave. It had a fringe of long icicles hanging down over it like a spiky curtain.

'It's in there, the human-boy thing,' said Squitcher. 'With Boldly Seer. We didn't know where else to put him to be safe...'

'Safe with a dragon?' squeaked Amy.

'Oh, yes. And she'll keep him warm too. She's named after one of your humans.'

'Is she? I don't think I've ever heard—'

'Not heard of Boldly Seer? She was a wild, fierce woman who rode in a chariot. She was a Queen. Our dragon's strong and brave like that.'

'Golly,' said Amy. She whispered to Copper, 'I think he means Boadicea, don't you?'

'Yeah.' Copper nodded. 'But I like Boldly Seer much better.'

From the cave they heard a dreadful wailing.

'*Woo woo aagh. Woo woo aagh.*'

'It's Boldly Seer,' said Squitcher. 'She's not at all jolly
– we don't know why.'

Boldly Seer was the size of a large African elephant.
She lay stretched out on the floor of the cave on her
tummy. She had a long delicate snout. Her flaring, pink-
spotted nostrils, like something from inside a sea
creature, were trembling. Her wings were folded neatly
to her sides. They reminded Amy of rather tatty, frilled
net curtains. The dragon's spiked ears, which probably
normally stood up, were laid back against her head.

She was crying.

'*Woo woo aagh. Woo woo aagh.*'

'That's why Grampy thinks a Dragon Destroyer
walked by,' said Squitcher. 'It's the sort of thing they do.
Terrible-bad.' He wiped a tear from his own eye.

The dragon gazed up at Copper and Amy hopefully.
Her tail twitched. She didn't lift her head from the
ground.

Amy slipped behind Copper. 'She's huge! And warm.
Can you feel the heat coming off her?'

'She is warmly-hot,' said Squitcher. 'That's why we
have to keep her out here away from the houses. She's a
good dragon. No need to be scared. She wouldn't hurt a
snowflake.' He sniffed and wiped a crystal dewdrop
from the end of his nose. 'Do you think you could help
and aid her...?'

Copper kneeled down at Boldly Seer's head. 'My
aunt has a dragon called Glinty. I'm not scared.' Very
gently she stroked the creature's soft, warm leathery
skin. It was mottled in a multitude of pinks, purples and

silver. 'She's like a gigantic rainbow trout, isn't she?'

'I can hear something,' said Amy. 'Something's snorting.'

'Oh, I am so forgetting-brainless!' cried Squitcher. He hit his forehead with his hand. 'Come and see it. Is your missing boy lanky? Tall as a two-year-old furzz tree? Does it have a brown fur on its head? And a long scarf round its neck-piece?'

Copper grinned at Amy. 'Yes! Where is he?'

17
How Questrid came to be on the Other Side

Questrid set out full of angry energy. He kept stopping
and listening, alert to any strange sounds in the still,
deadly calm of the white landscape.

Early on he had bashed his knee against a rock hidden
in the snow and it throbbed now. His toes were numb
because he hadn't had time to put on an extra pair of
socks.

He looked up the hill towards the blue of the mountain tops and down into the valley over the pine forests
and boulders below. There wasn't anything to see or
hear and yet still he felt uneasy.

He knelt down and sniffed. Ralick's wolfy scent hung
around, along with the strangely empty smell of Shane
Annigan. How can someone smell so strongly of
nothing? wondered Questrid. The scent of cold water.
Thin air.

He examined the marks in the snow. He was on the

right path. Shane barely touched the ground as he moved, but when he did, his long feet skidded through the top layer, leaving long soft marks. His cloak left a wide velvety trail.

Questrid picked up a handful of the snow and held it to his nose. He closed his eyes and inhaled deeply again. He concentrated every cell of his body on the odour.

Questrid had arrived at Spindle House when he was about six years old. It was Cedar who had noticed how Questrid stuck his nose into the air and sniffed, like a dog. The little boy searched out scents and studied animal marks left in the snow. They were clues to him.

'What bird made those prints?' Cedar asked the boy one day.

'Mistletoe Thrush,' said Questrid straight away.

'And those marks?'

'Black Squirrel.'

The boy did not speak for weeks after his arrival. He gave no clue to his name or whereabouts. Eventually the Beech family named him Questrid, the hunter. They found out later that his real name was Linden, but nobody ever called him that now – except sometimes his mother.

Questrid stood up and looked around slowly. Someone was watching him. Someone had just slipped out of sight the moment he'd turned round. He was certain of it.

He set off again, talking aloud to cheer himself along.

'I hope you're all right, Ralick. I know you're all right. Shane wouldn't hurt you, would he? He kept saying you were an interesting wolf cub, intelligent, special...Well, you are, Ralick. Copper loves you. I'm going to find you and bring you back.'

His hair felt hot and itchy under his hat, his scarf prickled his chin.

'Don't worry, Copper. I'm coming, Copper. You can trust me.'

Questrid came to the tunnel. He knew exactly what it was, a short cut to the valley on the other side. He knew it was tricky. He knew he might get through if he had the stamina and he might not get back. But that didn't matter if it meant he saved Ralick.

The scent of Ralick grew stronger.

Questrid came closer to the tunnel. He saw something lying in the snow beside the entrance. A rock? A sack? Or was it...His heart beat quickened. He ran.

Questrid scrambled up the last bit of the hill and flung himself onto the snow beside the cub.

'*Ralick!*'

Ralick was completely encased in a ball of gossamer thread – the same stuff Questrid had found clogging his door handle. The fine strands were wound round the cub's muzzle, his ears, his legs. The only things free to move were his eyes.

'Oh, Ralick!' Anger bubbled up inside him and he let out a yell of fury. 'Who did this? Shane Annigan? Was it?' He stopped. He sniffed the air like a dog. He could smell Shane Annigan. He was near. Very near...

'Questrid, my young friend, is it you?'

Shane Annigan jumped lightly down from a ledge

above the tunnel. A spume of light snowdust ballooned round him.

'Now, isn't it the nicest surprise to be meeting you here! Have you come far?' He dusted the snow from his arm.

'You know where I've come from!' cried Questrid. He leaped up and waved his fists at him. 'What've you done to Ralick?'

'Ah, my dear boy, it's a long story and one that I shan't trouble you with right now. I don't have the time. I haven't the inclination either.' He flicked the snow from his cloak. He grinned.

'You *will*! You must! I'm taking Ralick back right now and ...'

'Hush!' Shane's smile was overpowering. He was dazzling bright like a white fire. 'Hush now.'

'It's a trick, I know it is!' cried Questrid. He dived for Ralick.

'Look at this!' Shane commanded.

Questrid looked. He couldn't stop himself.

Shane held up his hand. Concealed in his palm was a ball of silver cobweb thread. He stretched out a finger and pointed straight at Questrid. A volley of shimmering iridescent lights, like white fireflies, shot from his finger.

Questrid was blinded. He didn't see the strands of fine thread that followed the lights. They floated through the air and fell over his head like a sparkling cobweb. He only felt a numbing calm descend on him and within seconds he'd dropped onto the snow. He lay there, cocooned in the silky filaments.

113

'There, there, my young friend,' said Shane Annigan. He smiled his creamy smile. 'You were after finding adventure. You found it!'

Shane quickly stuffed Ralick back into his sack and flung it over his shoulder. He grasped hold of Questrid and began to drag him into the tunnel. It took him only a matter of minutes to reach the other side. The dense air wasn't a problem for an Air person.

On the other side, Shane Annigan dumped Questrid on the snow.

'It's dangerous sleeping out on the mountainside in this inclement weather, young man,' he said. 'You might *die*!'

He walked leisurely away down the mountain.

Questrid lay in the snow for hours. He got colder and colder. He was quite blue by the time Squitcher found him.

The ice pixie bundled Questrid onto his sledge and took him home. The ice houses were too cold for a human, so Squitcher laid Questrid at the back of Boldly Seer's cave.

Dragons, and much around them, are always warm, if not hot.

18
Reunited

'Questrid!' Copper ran to the alcove. 'What's happened to him? He's covered in cobwebs!'

Squitcher and Copper knelt beside Questrid. 'He's not very jolly, is he? Snorting-groaning. Sleepy-mutterings. The same sort of magic is affecting Boldly Seer. Maybe Grampy is correctly-right. Maybe a Dragon Destroyer did come here.'

'Do Dragon Destroyers harm boys?' asked Copper. 'Oh, yes, they harm everything,' Squitcher assured her. 'It's their nature.'

Copper started to tug at the cobwebs. 'What is this stuff?' she said. 'Looks like cobwebs, but feels like nylon.'

'I tried too,' said Squitcher. 'But it's too powerful-strong for pixicles. Even my sharply-knife's not sharp enough.'

Copper sat back on her heels. 'This stuff makes me think of knitting,' she said. 'Of a great ball of fine, shiny

115

thread.' She grinned at Amy, who was standing apart, watching.

'What are you thinking, Coppery Girl?' asked Squitcher. He looked from Copper to Amy and back again. 'Is it magic? Jolly knitting magic?'

Copper nodded. She pulled off her backpack and dug around inside it. At last she reached the small knitting needles she'd hidden there. She flourished them.

'These are knitting needles. Remember I had one pair, Amy? Ruby gave me them. I kept them a secret from Mum. I can knit anything.'

Copper took up a free end of the fine thread and began winding it round her needles as if she were casting on stitches. The thread sprang into life as the needles touched it. It reared up like a wild, thin snake and wrapped itself round the metal knitting needles.

'Whoah!' cried Copper. The thread laced itself about, whipped and lashed through the air. Copper fought to keep it under control. 'I'm knitting worms!' she cried.

Copper's wrists flicked and bent. Her fingers danced. The cobwebs slithered off, tangling themselves into perfect stitches on her needles.

'Undoing Dragon Destroyer magic!' cried Squitcher. He jumped up and down. 'Bravo! Bravo!'

Amy was entranced. She watched Copper's fingers flying backwards and forwards and the thread turn from strands into fabric.

'I used to knit all the time.' Copper didn't look up. 'I used to feel weird unless I could knit, but this isn't quite like that... Doing this knitting makes me feel weird.'

116

Questrid began to wriggle. He pushed at the web. He was trying to speak. 'Shayannigun,' he said. 'Itwash Shayannigun.'

'*Shane Annigan! He* did this?' said Copper.

She knitted the last strands from around his chin and mouth.

'Yes!' Questrid shouted. 'He's a liar and a cheat. He locked me in my room. He's stolen Ralick—'

'He's stolen Ralick?'

'Yes.' Questrid sat up. 'I don't think Shane was ever lost in the storm. It was all a plot to get Ralick. I hate that man! Hey, how did you find me? It's great to see you.'

'Why would Shane want to steal Ralick?' Copper said. 'Why?'

'Don't know, but I *saw* him do it.'

'Magic cobwebs. Magic knitting,' cried Squitcher, hopping about. 'Very darkly-dangerous.'

'Questrid, this is Squitcher. He's an ice pixie and he saved you.'

'You were lying in the snow like a big caterpillar,' said Squitcher. 'So I brought you back here.'

'Thank you, Squitcher. You saved my life.'

'My enjoyable-pleasure. No more trouble than blowing a snowflake off a baby's bottom,' said Squitcher. 'Now, Coppery One, you must take care with that stuff you've made. Magic reworked is very strongly-powerful.'

'Can you knit *anything*?' asked Amy.

'Not really. Once I heard of someone who could knit gold!' Copper shared a secret smile with Questrid.

Amy noticed their private look. It hurt like a knife wound. 'Who could do that? Are they very rich?' she said.

'No, they're not,' said Copper. 'They decided it was too dangerous and stopped.'

'How could it be dangerous? If it was me, I'd never stop,' said Amy. 'If I could knit gold I'd do it all day and all night. Think how rich you could be!' Her eyes shone. She picked up a handful of snow and squeezed it into a hard ball. 'How could you have too much gold? You could buy TVs, clothes, houses...'

'Yes,' said Copper, 'but who needs more than one house? How many pairs of new shoes do you need and—'

'*Woo. Aaargh. Woo!*'

'And if you could make gold,' Amy said, 'you'd just make it all the time, wouldn't you? Every time you wanted something you could have it. Everyone would respect you. You'd be like a Queen...'

No one was listening to her. They were looking at the dragon. It had started wailing again.

'*Woo, woo!*'

'A dragon!' said Questrid. 'I've only just realised that's what that big silvery thing is! Golly. What an odd noise it makes.'

'That's Boldly Seer,' Copper told him. 'Squitcher thinks a Dragon Destroyer has harmed it... Shane said he loved dragons, but now I'm wondering...'

'He said lots of things!' said Questrid. 'Lies. I bet he is the Dragon Destroyer.'

Questrid went round and knelt down beside Boldly Seer. He stroked her head. 'She's beautiful. Is she gentle, Squitcher?'

'Most gentle-calm and usually very jolly,' said Squitcher sadly. 'Can you knit her back again, Coppery One?'

The dragon lifted her head and tossed it from side to side. Smoke swirled around them and little sparks of hot ash fell sizzling into the snow.

Amy kept against the wall.

'Isn't she a bit of a hazard?' asked Questrid. 'I mean, she's so hot and, well, you're all so cold!'

Squitcher smiled. He laid his tiny white hand on the dragon's nose.

'Not a hazard, never. Oh dear, her nose is wet and cold. So not well.' He shook his head. 'What's the matter, Boldly Seer? Speak to us. Tell us and we'll help you. We cannot do without our dear-lovely dragon.'

'So she doesn't melt everything?'

'No. She hotly-fires the giant blocks of ice, you know. She blazes it into smaller cubes, so we can lift it. When we're building a new house, you should see her blow it all smooth-sheeny. Jolly brilliant. She takes us places too. We need her.'

Suddenly, the dragon began to shift. Everyone got out of the way. She flung herself over onto her back with her legs in the air. She whacked her head against the earth as if it were hurting. She let out a long, muffled, deep cry.

When she half-opened her mouth and roared, they caught sight of a flash of silver.

119

'Cobwebs in her mouth!' Questrid said. 'Shane Annigan at work again!'

Squitcher gently lifted the dragon's lips and peeled them back revealing the delicate rose-pink inner skin. There was silvery thread wrapped around her tongue and teeth. 'Yes, yes,' he said. 'You are so right. Everywhere. Poor, dear, Boldly Seer.'

'Let me see what I can do,' said Copper. She took out her needles and began to try and knit it off, but the needles were too long. Even with her elbows pointing up to the ceiling, she could not knit it.

'I just can't get them in! It's so frustrating,' she said. 'There isn't room. If only I had a—'

'*Crochet hook!*' said Questrid. 'I knew you'd be glad of it! I have one of yours, right here in my pocket.'

'You don't? Questrid, that's amazing!' said Copper.

Smarty pants! Amy thought. Why didn't I bring something useful? Why can't I help? Why do they keep grinning at each other, like they've got whole mountains of secrets? It's not fair. It's just not fair!

'Crochet hooks are very useful – I unpicked a lock with one once, you know,' said Copper. 'From now on I shall never leave home without one.'

'Who locked you up?' asked Squitcher.

'Granite,' said Copper grimly.

Amy squirmed.

Copper was almost lying on the floor beside the dragon. Gently she eased the tiny hook between Boldly Seer's lips. She began to slip the thread off the pointed teeth.

'This is like French knitting,' said Copper. She giggled. 'Poof! What does this dragon eat? Her breath is awful...Here it comes...It's coming off, it's crocheting itself... It's going soft and silky.'

Boldly Seer lay very still. She did not blink her eyes, but stared at Copper intently. At last Copper finished.

'There!' She stood up. 'All done.'

The dragon suddenly let out a great whoosh of smoke. Everyone jumped out of the way and flung themselves against the walls. Boldly Seer flexed her legs, rolled over and got onto her feet.

Standing up she was enormous. She tossed her head backwards and forwards. She flapped her wings. She smacked her lips together. Sparks shot out of her nose and mouth. Smoke filled the air.

Amy was sheltering on the other side of the cave to the others. The two abandoned silky squares lay in a patch of snow. And the crochet hook. Quickly she picked them up. The knitted fabric was glossy and slippery. It reminded her of the inside of seashells. She slipped everything into her pocket. The pixicle said magic reworked was more powerful. Well. I might just need these, thought Amy. You never know... She went round the dragon to join the others.

'Boldly is so happy-jolly,' squeaked Squitcher. He was leaping around to avoid the shower of burning sparks and the dragon's thrashing tail. 'Thank you so jolly much. Hold still there, Boldly! Be careful!' He sidled nearer to Copper. 'You must have food and gift-rewards—' He stopped. 'But what rewards? We have

121

nothing here for humans...Oh dear, oh dear...I know!
I will allow you to see into my eye-cycle as a reward.
This is, in case you don't know, a finely-wonderful and
rare reward.'

'See into your icicles?' said Amy. 'Why?'

'No, no, *eye-cycles*,' said Squitcher. 'Come. I'll show
you.'

Outside the cold made Copper and Questrid start
shivering. Boldly Seer had kept the cave very warm and
cosy.

Squitcher led them to the nearerst ice house. He
pointed into the garden. 'That's an eye-cycle.'

'I thought they were sculptures,' said Amy.

'You're very right!' laughed Squitcher clapping his
hands. 'E-y-e-c-y-c-l-e-s...'he spelt it out for them. 'It
is arty. And is jolly good prediction machine also. You
look through them and you see things.'

'What things?' Amy was suddenly nervous.

'It depends. Cycles go round and round-a-bout so it
could be forward or back,' said Squitcher. 'We use the
eye-cycles to answer questions.'

'Like fortune tellers?' said Questrid.

'Yes, you could call us that. Pastune tellers too. They
work both ways. I'm thinking it would be jolly useful to
be able to see what the Shane Annigan person is doing.
And where he has taken the Ralick.'

'Fantastic idea,' said Copper. 'Will they do that?'

'Might do...But not now,' said Squitcher. 'Too late
and not enough light. First, we must get you food and
make places for you to sleep and all those things.

Humans are too big for fitting into the ice houses, so we will bring everything out to the cave. Please wait.'

Squitcher soon reappeared with six other pixicles. They brought mattresses and blankets. The mattresses were so small that they needed two each to lie on. The pixicles brought food too. It wasn't very tasty, being so cold, but it made them feel much better once they'd eaten it.

The other pixicles were shy and did not stay and talk. Squitcher said goodnight and went back to his ice house. Soon all the lights went out and it was quiet.

Questrid and Copper laid their mattresses down at the back of the cave. Amy put hers nearer the entrance of the cave where it was cooler. Boldly Seer was curled up like a giant cat against the wall, snoring.

'Listen to her tummy!' Questrid said. 'It sounds like a crowd of people are striking matches in there.'

'Are you OK over there, Amy?' said Copper.

'I'm fine.'

'I hope everyone back home isn't too worried about us,' said Questrid.

'They'll have got Casimir's message,' said Copper. 'They know what we're doing...I hope Ralick's all right.'

Amy stared into the darkness and dug her fingers into the snow beside her. She made a snowball. She punched eyes into it. A mouth. Made a nose.

She looked out through the mouth of the cave at the black sky. It was dotted with stars. She listened to the dragon's belly gurgling and bubbling. She listened to her breathing. Perhaps Copper couldn't sleep either. This would be such a good moment to speak to her, to tell her the truth. In the dark.

'Copper? Copper?' she called softly.

But both Copper and Questrid had fallen asleep.

Amy sighed.

Something hot fell on her cheek. It was a tear. But it couldn't be! I don't weep, she thought. I'm strong. She wiped it away and rubbed her damp nose...

Her nose. Her *face*. She'd almost forgotten those awful things the rockgoyle had said. Now she remembered. What if my face is going ugly and spoiling like that rockgoyle told me? she thought. I haven't seen a mirror for ages. Copper's too nice to say. Squitcher wouldn't know...Did Questrid look at me oddly? Maybe I'm getting uglier and uglier and everyone knows what a cheat I am and hates me.

I wish I'd never come. I wish I'd never seen Granite, or Malachite Mountain or Copper or anything.

19
The Eye-Cycles

Squitcher woke them in the morning. He brought glasses of a delicious red juice and white cake with pink icing. After they had eaten, they went outside.

All the other pixicles were watching them from the windows or the doors of their houses.

Every single pixicle was wearing a brightly coloured hat.

'Hats because it's a great privilege-honour to use the eye-cycles,' explained Squitcher. He was wearing a sky blue hat with ear flaps. 'Come on.'

He led them to his house. There was an eye-cycle in the garden. It was carved from a solid cloudy stack of ice. It was like a totem pole, patterned with faces and animals.

'It's beautiful,' said Copper. 'I love the noise it makes when the chimes jangle.'

'*Tune*,' Squitcher said. He stroked the eye-cycle

125

proudly. 'Fortunes and pastunes. Presently this is singing-ringing a pastune. Just what you need, I think.'

At the height of Copper's knee – eye level for a pixicle – there was a cross-piece. It was angled through the main pole. This was the bit you looked through, like a telescope.

'No promises,' said Squitcher, anxiously. 'Might not be working today for you. Also might not understand what you see. Put your right eye against the hole,' he said. 'Close other eye and sort of think about what you want to know.'

Copper did as he said. 'Oh, it's blowing cold air at me!' She laughed. 'Can't see a thing... It's all dark, no... here it comes... it's clearing... I'm seeing something!'

Amy watched anxiously. She bit her lip.

What if Copper's pastune showed Amy speaking with Granite? Amy carving horrible gargoyles down in the basement with Aunt Agnes and Uncle John? What if it showed Amy choking on the smell of wood? Or leaning out of the window to eavesdrop on Copper and Questrid?

Amy busied herself with the ball of snow. It was somehow still in her hands from last night. She was finishing its features. It was soothing to work on it while she watched.

The eye-cycle began to make a tune. It began to whisper and tinkle. The sound reminded Amy of hailstones falling on ice. Wind murmuring through the pine trees. Cold water trickling.

'Pastune arriving!' said Squitcher. He clapped his hands. 'Pictures coming!'

Amy felt hot blood flooding her cheeks. They are going to find out about me! It's not fair, it's not fair! She concentrated on her snowball face. She gave it some heavy eyebrows. Some big fangs. It wasn't as simple as it used to be, somehow. The chin crumbled and fell...I haven't had a chance. Everything's spoiled now. I hate them...

Copper was speaking slowly. 'Yes, yes...' she said. 'I see Shane Annigan. He's smirking. He's got Ralick. Ralick's there! He's all tied up with that stuff. Like Questrid. They're going through big white doors, really big doors... The walls are sort of greenish and slippery. It's got windows like the Rock. Now I see it's a mountain. There's a crystal ball thing on the top – and, oh! It's gone!'

'Where?' said Questrid. He peered over Copper's shoulder, trying to see into the eye-cycle. 'I want to see!'

Squitcher rubbed his little pointed ears. 'Sounds like Malachite Mountain to me.'

Malachite Mountain? Amy let go of the snowball face she'd made. It dropped into the snow with a 'plop'. What was Shane Annigan doing *there*?

'What's the matter, Amy?' said Copper.

Questrid picked up Amy's snowball. 'Here you go. Don't spoil your snow sculpture.'

Amy tried to snatch the ball back from him. 'Leave it alone.'

'Sorry...Oh, it's a face,' said Questrid. He gave it a

127

long look. 'Amy, it's scary! What on earth made you do that!' He held it up for the others to see. 'Look! Isn't it freaky?'

The face had heavy brows and protruding frog eyes which somehow, even made out of snow, were full of hatred. The mouth seemed to be laughing meanly. It managed to look more evil without a chin.

'Amy, how could you?' said Copper.

Amy snatched it back. She threw it away with all her might. 'I don't know,' she shouted. 'I didn't mean to. It just grew. I didn't know it was so ugly. Don't look at me like that! It was nothing!'

'I think it's very clever,' said Squitcher. 'You'd make fine ice sculptor. Make good eye-cycles.'

'Forget it,' said Amy. 'Just forget it.'

She saw Copper and Questrid exchange a bemused glance. Her insides hurt.

'The Malaknight Mountain, then?' Amy said. She thrust her hands into her pockets and assumed an innocent expression. 'Is it near?'

'Mala*chite*,' Squitcher said. 'It's not far, as the dragon flies. Granite lives-abiding there now.'

'*Granite?*' Copper squeaked. 'Ah, yes. That's where Lord Lazulite lived, isn't it? And Granite took over. But what has Shane Annigan got to do with Granite? I don't understand . . .'

'Would it be all right if I tried one of the eye-cycles?' asked Amy. 'Just quickly?'

'Of course you may,' said Squitcher. 'You have been helping also. It's singing a fortune now.'

128

Amy knelt down in the snow and put her eye against the round eye hole. Cold damp air blew against her eyeball. She blinked. The darkness cleared and she saw her room at Malachite Mountain. She gasped. She could see herself there, in the future! It was her, Amy! She was wearing the new pale blue, fur-lined cloak with the hood that Granite had given her. The figure turned very slowly. Amy's blood froze. The hairs on the back of her neck prickled. Her face! Her face had changed. It had changed like the rockgoyle said it would. It was the face of the ugliest, grey-skinned, pointy-eared rockgoyle she'd ever seen.

'No!' She sat down heavily. 'No! It's not true! It's not!' Copper rushed to her. 'What is it?'

But Amy shook her head. 'Nothing, nothing,' she croaked weakly. 'Just a surprise. Someone I didn't expect to see. Nothing.'

'Remember, Amy, that you don't always see so truly-clearly if it is the future you look into,' whispered Squitcher. 'It is not so solid. Hasn't yet happened like the gone-away-past.'

'Oh, no, this was clear,' said Amy, grimly. 'Couldn't be clearer.'

I'm turning into a rockgoyle, she thought, and nothing will stop it. I've seen it happen! There's no hope for me, no hope. I might as well be horrid and mean because I'm turning into the ugliest creature in the universe, anyway.

'Poor Amy,' said Copper. 'Perhaps you should have looked at a pastune, not a fortune?'

129

Amy bit back hard words that sprang to her lips. Leave me alone, she wanted to scream at them. Don't be nice to me! You don't know what I am. You have no idea what's happening to me! She turned her back on them.

'Now I'm thinking speed is important,' said Squitcher. 'Jolly far-distant away that Malachite Mountain and you need to be there. Yes?'

'Yes,' said Copper. She was lingering close to Amy. Amy knew Copper wanted to comfort her, but she kept her back to her.

'And you tell me this Shane Annigan did that thing to Boldly Seer and to your lanky boy and stole your wolf?'

'Yes,' said Copper.

'Then he is Dragon Destroyer. Enemy. Maybe Boldly Seer will take us there.'

'Great!' cried Questrid. 'Oh, fantastic! I've *always* wanted to ride a dragon. Oh, will she? Really?'

'Let's go ask her,' said Squitcher.

Amy followed them slowly back to the cave. If only she had a mirror. She tried to feel her cheeks and nose to see if they'd changed, but it was so hard to tell. And anyway, she hadn't got time to dwell on her face. It was Shane and Granite that she needed to concentrate on.

Shane Annigan must have known I was going to kidnap Ralick, she thought. But he got the wolf first. *He* wants the reward. Granite'll be so angry and disappointed with me! He won't make me a princess. He won't let me stay at Malachite Mountain. I don't want to go back to Aunt Agnes and Uncle John. It's not fair.

130

Boldly Seer was pottering around in the group of furzz trees behind the cave, stripping off the young leaves and munching them. She snorted with pleasure when she saw them coming and flapped her wings, sending the loose snow whirling around in a mini blizzard.

'Whoa!'cried Squitcher. 'Gently does it, Boldly, dear.'

'Awesome!' Questrid gazed up at her, grinning. She towered over them.

'Isn't she beautiful?' said Copper. 'Her skin's like fish scales, only softer. And she's so shiny. Those lovely lacy wings.'

Squitcher said something in dragon-speak. The dragon closed her wings and put her large head down beside his tiny one, listening. Squitcher reached on tiptoe and whispered into her ear.

'Boldly Seer's jolly about it,' he said. 'She'll take us.'

Three red and blue-hatted pixicles appeared with a large saddle. Two pixicles, one in a green hat and one in a yellow hat, brought a ladder and set it up against Boldly Seer's side. It took two more pixicles to fix the saddle and harness onto the dragon's back and buckle the girth.

'Specially made,' Squitcher told them. 'Made for Boldly Seer. No other dragon just this back-size, this back-shape.'

The saddle had four seats. Each seat had straps and harnesses to hold the passengers in place.

'No reins?' asked Questrid. He was used to strapping his horses to their sledge and was looking forward to steering Boldly Seer.

131

'Outrageous-rude suggestion,' squeaked Squitcher. 'She is dragon Queen and needs no reins. Just much respect. All aboard!' he shouted. 'All aboard for a jolly adventure! Watch out for her whirlings and upside-down flyings,' he said. 'Buckle up! Also watch out for he-dragons. Boldly seeks a mate.'

'Blimey!' said Questrid. He sat down and pulled his straps round tightly.

'Did he say upside down?' whispered Copper.

Squitcher tied the flaps of his blue hat down firmly and buckled his straps. 'Here we go!' he called.

He leaned forward and spoke to the dragon.

As soon as Boldly Seer heard his words, she lifted herself up onto her toes. Her massive wings burst apart with a loud, papery sound. She surged forward and broke into a run. She didn't run smoothly, but like a lolloping camel, throwing her passengers from side to side. Amy couldn't stop a little scream escaping. Boldly Seer beat her wings; they thrashed and flapped like tents in a gale. Snow swirled into the air. The ground rushed by.

'One, two, three!' cried Squitcher.

With a tremendous whoosh and surge of muscle, Boldly Seer rose into the air.

'Yahoo!' cried Questrid.

Amy gripped the sides of her seat until her fingers hurt. She squeezed her lips together tightly. She looked down and saw the pixicles cheering and waving their coloured hats in the air. It looked for a moment like it was raining giant smarties.

Boldly Seer flew straight up over the hillside, tilting over the white houses. Then she swerved and cut out across the valley. There was suddenly more and more space between them and the ground. They were very high.

The rushing air was filled with the sound of Boldly Seer's wings; a sound like a paper kite filling with air and throbbing against the air currents. With each beat of her wings, Amy felt the dragon's muscles working and her body stretching and bending beneath her.

The distant mountains were tinged with colour, as if someone had spilled pink, orange, purple and red paint over them. The colours were reflected in Boldly Seer's wings; they flashed like giant butterflies.

'This is wonderful!' Questrid shouted.

'Good. Sky very jolly,' cried Squitcher.

Every now and then, rumbling, gurgling sounds rippled out of the dragon. Amy felt them vibrating through her legs. Each gurgle was followed by a snort, billowing smoke and sparks.

Boldly Seer climbed higher and higher.

'I am so definitely going to be a Dragon-Master when I'm older,' Questrid shouted into Amy's ear. 'Isn't this fantastic!'

Amy nodded. She closed her eyes. She couldn't enjoy it. She was worried. What was going to happen? She wanted to conjure up the wonderful feeling she'd got when she first came to Malachite Mountain. She needed to feel important again. Wanted. But now all she could see when she closed her eyes was Copper with Ralick bounding through the snow behind her. Or Copper and

133

Ralick whispering secrets to each other. Or Copper and Questrid on the lake, laughing. And Amy, always on the edge. Alone.

The other vivid picture she couldn't get out of her head was the dreadful fortune she'd seen. That was etched into her brain as if chemically burnt into it. Please don't let it come true... If only I could see my face. If only I had a mirror.

She remembered that Uncle John had said Granite was horrid on the outside because he was nasty on the inside. Is that like me? If I was nicer maybe I won't end up ugly. Maybe I could tell Copper the truth. Really tell her. But will she ever forgive me?

They passed over the town of Antimakassar – a city of tall towers and a mighty castle. They swooped over a vast forest and along a valley. Then in the distance, they saw a glimmer of the strange green sheen of Malachite Mountain. Almost immediately clouds closed over it and it slipped from view.

'Bad weather up ahead,' called Squitcher. 'Not very jolly I think.'

He was right. Minutes later, instead of the warm, bright sunshine, they found themselves flying into a dense, thick and clammy fog. It clung wetly to their clothes. They could not see anything further than an arm's-length away.

Boldy Seer slowed down.

'Don't worry!' Squitcher called. 'Dragon has internal radar... but landing might be bone-rattling-bumpy.'

Amy felt Copper reach out and squeeze her arm

reassuringly. She wished she was the sort of person to respond with a word and a squeeze back. But she wasn't. She couldn't.

They flew onwards into the cloudy sky. Thick grey fog swirled round them. Sometimes it was so dense that they couldn't see their own hands in front of their faces.

'Coming down to ground-landing!' called Squitcher. 'Hold on. Brace! Brace!'

There was a massive jolt and thud as Boldly Seer hit the ground. Snow flew up over them. The dragon slithered, wings outstretched, and ploughed through the snow for twenty metres until she stopped.

'Not bad,' said Squitcher. 'Everyone jolly? No hurtings?'

'I'm fine. Where are we?' said Copper.

'Can't see a thing,' said Questrid. 'Or maybe I can see some trees and of course some snow.'

'We'll all be jolly in a very few minutes, you'll see,' said Squitcher. 'Stay where you are ... ' He unbuckled his straps and slipped out of his seat down into the snow. 'Back in a minute.'

Whirling fog obliterated everything. They sat in silence. The dragon tossed her head and panted. Amy felt her leathery sides going in and out like a concertina beneath her.

'Did you hear something?' said Questrid. 'I definitely *heard* something ... '

'Me too ... ' said Copper.

Now Amy heard it too. Something was howling.

It sounded like wolves.

20
Wolfgang

'Great,' said Questrid. 'We're in fog thicker than mud, surrounded by wolves and our guide's abandoned us.'

He slithered down from his seat. He patted Boldly Seer's flank. 'Thanks, Boldly Seer. That was great. I'd love to do that all over again. Come on down, you two.'

'Is it safe?' asked Amy. 'Is that really wolves?' She slithered down with Copper. They stood in a huddle beside the dragon.

'Yes, I think it is,' said Questrid. 'Look, there's a light!'

'Hello! Hello again,' called Squitcher. 'Come this way. Wolfgang Zomart's ready to welcome you in. Come.'

Copper took Amy's arm. They followed Questrid towards the light.

'I must settle Boldly Seer down to rest. Wolfgang has snugly-warm cave round the back for her,' said Squitcher. 'You go with Wolfgang.'

136

They couldn't see Wolfgang in the thick hazy fog, but they heard him. He had a very heavy accent. 'Come this way,' he said, only it sounded like: *Kom ziss vay.* 'Don't mind the wolves.' He pronounced it *volves.* 'They'll soon settle. Don't mind them. Come.'

Wolfgang was standing at his open door. A welcoming yellow light shone out onto the snow. The wolves weren't howling now, they were making yipping noises and barking. It still sounded scary.

'*Ze Zanctuary,*' said Wolfgang, spreading his arm out to show them.

'He means Sanctuary, I think,' said Copper, quietly.

Wolfgang's skin was the colour and texture of a walnut. It was very brown and lined, from being out in the sun, Amy guessed, rather than from being old. His hair was bushy and streaked with grey. He had a wiry, grizzled beard which reached down to his waist. The whites of his eyes were the whitest she'd ever seen. He smiled round at them, nodding gently, and when he came to Amethyst, seemed to linger, studying her.

Amy squirmed. She was worried he had seen something unpleasant.

Squitcher came in. 'I've settled Boldly Seer,' he told them. 'She's sleepily-tired. Oh, Wolfgang, it's jolly hot in here! I'll melt in this heat.'

'I didn't know the ice visitor was coming,' laughed Wolfgang. 'Come in. Sit down, everyone. The friends of the Squitcher's is a friends of mine.' He pronounced Squitcher, *Skvitsher.*

137

Wolfgang's house was made of leather and wood, iron and stone all put together in a higgledy-piggledy way. A massive log fire burned in a great brick-lined fireplace. Pierced metal lanterns hung from the ceiling and from brackets on the walls, making sharply-patterned shadows on the surfaces, like black snowflakes. The floor was carpeted with reeds and strips of bark, pine needles and rushes.

The wolves were very close. Amy could hear them pacing back and forwards and whimpering.

'What sort of a sanctuary is it?' asked Questrid.

'One for pixicles and humans,' said Squitcher, with a chuckle.

'For wolves,' said Wolfgang. 'For all ones needing it, too.' Amy was sure he gave her a particular look as he said that.

'We're grateful,' said Copper. 'We're on our way to Malachite Mountain. To find my wolf cub, Ralick.'

'Not in this weather,' said Wolfgang. 'Not possible. You fall down the crevasse, you fall down the ravine. You wait till the fog is cleared away.'

'We can't!' cried Copper. 'I've got to find Ralick!'

'No even find Malachite Mountain in this fog,' said Wolfgang. 'Rest first. Maybe it clear in two hours. Maybe it clear in five minutes. Can tell never.'

'He's right, Coppery One,' said Squitcher. 'Know it's not jolly, but it's best you do as he says.'

'Besides,' said Wolfgang, 'visitors is rare. Come see wolves. Put minds at rest.'

Wolfgang unlatched the door alongside the fireplace.

It led straight through to a large barn.

'Wow!' Questrid said.

They flattened themselves against the barn wall.

'Wow!'

There was a whole pack of wolves in the barn. They were padding backwards and forwards inside a fenced-off area. They bunched together and fixed their yellow eyes on the visitors.

The smell of the wolves was intense and pungent. Amy held her nose. There were half-gnawed bones on the floor amongst the sawdust. The air was cold.

'Seven darlings need sanctuary at the moment,' Wolfgang told them. 'I find them injured or alone. I am bringing them here. Oh! Copper! Not too close! They're dangerous!'

'Of course they are,' said Copper, quickly stepping away from the barrier. 'I forgot. You see we've got tame ones at home.'

'These wolves know only the mountains,' said Wolfgang, rubbing at his beard. 'They are wild. I feed them and care for them, but they'd take me for the *zandvitch* filling if I was careless.'

The seven wolves resumed pacing backwards and forwards on their big broad feet. Wolfgang started to describe their eating patterns and their particular habits and dislikes. Amy slipped back into the other room; she could not even pretend to be interested like Copper was.

Squitcher was sitting beside the open door fanning his pale face. Fog drifted in, then disappeared as it warmed.

He grinned at Amy. 'Too stifling-hot,' he said.

139

'Me too.' Amy scooped up a handful of snow from beside the door and smoothed it over her cheeks. 'I long for ice and flatness. Crystals and stone.'

'All there in Malachite Mountain, dear Rock girl, if that'll make you jolly,' said Squitcher. His eyes twinkled. For a moment Amy wondered if he was being sarcastic, but his pale blue eyes were gentle.

'Yes,' she replied. She sat beside him. 'It is, I suppose.'

Squitcher's little face was so kind, so open and trusting...

'Squitcher, can I tell you something?' she said. 'Ask you something?'

'Of course. How jolly!' Squitcher sat up and clasped his hands over his knee, head on one side. 'Ready-waiting.'

'Squitcher, I am not a good person—'

'Hah, that is not at all truly-honest!' said Squitcher. 'I see you being sad-unhappy, but you are not bad. You are helping your friend Coppery One. You are looking for her Ralick. You are a good girl.'

'I want to be, but Squitcher... I started out with such bad intentions.'

'That is a shame,' said Squitcher. He put his tiny hand on her larger one and patted her. 'But that's how you started out, you say, and need not be how you continue. You start out one way, change your mind and alter course-directions. Why not? Boldy Seer goes thisaway, thataway, all the time. Wind changes, the way looks bleak, off she goes.'

Amy felt a little surge of hope. 'Do you really think it's possible?'

'I jolly well do.'

'Thank you. I think, then, there is a chance for me. I can try.'

'You can try,' said Squitcher. 'You will jolly well try and you jolly well will be jolly!'

The fog hung around the house. Nothing was visible through the windows and no sound from outside reached them.

Wolfgang served everyone a bowl of chunky soup and warm bread that he had baked himself. Those that liked the warmth, sat around the fire. The others sat further away. Wolfgang told them stories about wolves and dragons and things that lived deep in the mountains.

One by one, the listeners dropped asleep.

Squitcher lay along the bottom of the front door in the cold air which seeped underneath it. His snores rattled the door on its hinges.

Amy woke before anyone else. Her sleep had been full of nasty dreams. She opened her eyes, but didn't move. There was light outside, no sunshine, but the fog had lifted. Amy could see the surrounding forest and Malach-ite Mountain about a mile away through the window.

I could go now, she thought, before anyone else is awake. I could rescue Ralick . . . I wish . . . I wish . . . Her fingers closed around the cobweb squares that Copper had made. She pulled one out from her pocket and held it up to the light. It was just like a cobweb, only stronger and with an extra silky quality. If only it was really magic, she thought, if only it would do something useful and help me . . .

'Eeek, eek.'

'Rat!' She sat up. 'Hello. Shh, don't squeak too loudly. Don't wake anyone. Where did you come from? How did you find me?'

She slipped the cobweb square into her pocket again: had it brought her friend to her? Was it magic?

'Pss, pss.'

He seemed to be smiling at her; certainly he was showing his yellow teeth. His nose was twitching.

But was he a friend? He was Granite's rat. Could he be a friend?

There was a message in the white cylinder tied around his tummy. Her fingers were trembling as she took it out. She smoothed it and read it.

'*Come.*' That was all it said. No *please* or well done for trying or anything. Just *come*.

Her heart sank. Granite was so cold! So bossy! So . . .

Granite doesn't care for me at all! She threw the note on the floor. He never has. He just wanted to use me.

All right. I'll do the same to him.

'I'll go to him, I will,' she whispered to the rat. 'And I'll pretend to be the old Amy, but inside, I'll be the new, rebellious Amy. That'll show them all.'

The rat bit her sleeve and tugged.

'And I suppose we'll find out whose side you're on too,' she said. 'Now, wait, just a minute.'

142

Amy glanced over at Questrid and Copper. They slept so peacefully. What would they think if she disappeared? She glanced at the window. It was getting brighter all the time. The light would surely wake them soon.

'Pss, pss!'

'Shh, wait.'

What does it matter anyway? she thought. They'll find out I've lied. They'll never forgive me. Still... She quickly wrote a note saying she had gone to Malachite Mountain on her own. To get Ralick. *I know a secret way in*, she lied. *Don't worry about me.*

As if they would.

Amy was halfway across the room when she spotted Squitcher. He was lying at the bottom of the front door like a draft excluder. She couldn't go that way.

The wolf barn! There must be a door at the other side of that. There had to be, otherwise how did Wolfgang get the wolves in and out? He wouldn't bring them through the cabin.

She turned back, tiptoed across the room, lifted the latch on the door very softly and went into the barn.

The smell of the creatures hit her. She pinched her nose. Ugh, it was awful.

The wolves all turned to her. She stood very still. They focused their strange cross-eyed eyes on her. They held their heads down low. Their tails did not move. One of them growled.

Amy swallowed loudly. Too dangerous, she thought. There *was* a door on the other side, but she'd have to walk right through them...

143

The white rat, who had taken up a position on her shoulder, nibbled her earlobe encouragingly. He tugged on her plait.

'OK, OK,' she whispered. 'Whose side are you on, anyway?'

No choice, then.

She climbed very slowly over the fence and began to edge round the pen. The wolves fixed her with their yellow eyes. They moved like a shoal of fish, like one being ... towards her.

She stopped; they stopped.

The white rat tugged at her hair again.

'It's all right for you,' she whispered. 'Up there ... But I'm scared.'

Keeping her back to the wall, she inched further round the barn. She never let her eyes lose contact with the wolves. She knew if she did that they would pounce.

The door was almost within reach. She turned away to open it. The wolves rushed.

They came at her in a growling, brown furry wave. She couldn't scream. She dare not risk a noise. She flung herself at the door, praying it wouldn't be locked.

Just as her hands touched the door, it fell open.

Wolfgang.

'What the ... !' exclaimed Wolfgang. 'Quick! This way!' He kicked the door shut and pulled her out of the way. They crashed to the floor. Crates of food, sacks of flour and packs of beans tumbled down around them. They were in a small storeroom. Large dry hams and bunches of dry herbs hung from the ceiling. The white rat scampered over the sacks. It squeezed under the door to the outside and in a flash it was gone.

'Amy! What are you doing coming through the wolf barn?'

'I don't know. I just—' Amy shook off his helping hand and stood up.

'Is dangerous! Why? Why? This is not the way out!' He got up too. He looked at her intently. 'Ah, sneaking away, is that it? While your comrades sleep? What do I tell them, later, eh?' said Wolfgang. 'What?'

Amy tossed her hair. She shrugged. 'Tell them what you like. I can do what I like,' she said. 'I don't care.'

Wolfgang glared at her. 'You are not like them,' he said at last. 'You are the loner like me. You do what you want? I say you outcast more like. Am I right?' He touched her arm gently.

Amy felt tears fill her eyes. She brushed them away angrily.

'No. I'm not. I was. Granite sent me to steal Ralick, but—'

'Whoah! So that's it!' Wolfgang let go of her arm as if she were contaminated. His eyes narrowed and he jerked his chin in the direction of Malachite Mountain. 'You can't know how bad that Granite is. You wouldn't do anything for that man if you heard the howling and shrieking I've heard.'

'Who? What?'

'A wolf cub. Nothing like the cry of a wolf in sadness. Didn't want to tell Copper. But when she told me about her Ralick, I knew.'

145

Amy shivered. In her mind's eye she saw the little wolf cub sitting on Copper's lap, staring lovingly up into Copper's face.

'And there's other badness there too. From the air,' said Wolfgang.

Amy shivered.

'Yes. Shane Annigan. The Will-o'-the-Wisp.' He pronounced it *Ze Vill of ze Visp*. 'Bad like disease. You cannot see it, is like germs, invisible. Getting into every nook and cranny.'

'Yes. I think I knew I was on the wrong side right from the beginning,' said Amy, 'but once I'd started, there seemed no way back.'

'I'm sorry for you, Amy, all alone—'

'I—'

'The wolves don't trust you, do they? Can smell something's not right. They know—'

'It's not my fault,' Amy snapped. 'I just spoil things. That's what I do...What I *used* to do, but now I'm going back to Granite and I'm going to put it all right. Truly I am.'

'Good, good.' Wolfgang rubbed his hands together. 'You have made good choice,' Wolfgang said. 'You have a choice, Amy, always, even if this time, is coming a bit late...'

Amy yanked the door open and ran out into the snow.

'Won't you wait for Copper?' called Wolfgang.

'I can't!' Amy called. 'I have to go!'

She ran. She did not turn back.

There was a path between the dense fir trees. The

146

snow was not very deep. It was soft and slushy and grey.

She didn't stop until she heard a sudden squeak. The white rat was perched on a log, waiting for her.

'There you are!' she said. 'How did you get here? Looking after number one, eh? At least you like me.' She bent down and let him jump up onto her arm. He scampered up to her shoulder. 'Or you pretend to.'

The rat snuggled against her neck. She liked the tickle of his fur against her skin. She even liked his scratchy little toes.

'I like you. You're my friend, aren't you?'

The rat purred.

'I'll take that as a yes.'

Amy went on. Malachite Mountain was due west. She did not need a guide: its green shining mass seemed to be the only thing she could see.

'*Nothing like the cry of a wolf in distress*,' Wolfgang had said. She didn't want to remember that, but the more she tried to forget, the louder and fiercer his words echoed in her head.

21
Return to Malachite Mountain

The fog had almost cleared, only a few wisps lingered like long, drifting scarves among the fir trees when Amy reached Malachite Mountain. The sun was shining, it made the mountain glitter and sparkle as if thousands of emeralds were embedded in its ice sides.

Amy went up the steps to the great white front door.

Her heart was pounding. She wiped her sweaty hands down her trousers. How am I going to hide my feelings? How can I pretend I still like him? I am mad!

A rockgoyle opened the door for her. It gave her a hard, bleak stare.

'What's the matter?' snapped Amy. She touched her face quickly. 'Something wrong?'

'No, Miss Amethyst,' said the rockgoyle. It looked down at its vast feet demurely.

'Good.' She pushed past it into the hall. 'Get me some food and an iced drink.' Her voice echoed in the emptiness. 'Is Granite in there?'

'Yes, Miss Amethyst.'

Amy sighed. How was it that *Miss Amethyst* sounded so utterly horrible all of a sudden? Like an insult.

She went into the Reception (*Deception* – perhaps the rockgoyle had been right) Chamber. The white rat jumped off her shoulder and onto a marble statue. It squeaked goodbye and went scampering up the stairs.

Alone again. Amy stood up as tall as she could. I'm the old Amy. I'm a princess. I'm cold, I'm hard and I care only for money, she told herself.

She went in.

Granite was slumped in a chair by the fire.'Hello, Amethyst,' he drawled. 'Told you she'd be here today, Shane.'

Shane. He was there. Amy stared at the pale man. He gleamed like a pearl. He was sitting at the table, sipping a fizzing blue drink. He smoothed his pale hair back over his head so it clung to his skull like a wave streaming over a rock.

'Amethyst.' He inclined his head towards her. 'Now, isn't this a pleasant surprise for sure.'

Amy went over to Granite. 'I tried my best,' she said. 'Honestly I did. But *he* stole the wolf cub before I got a chance to.' She pointed at Shane. 'He sneaked in and stole it! It wasn't my fault.'

Granite's face split into a big grin. He roared with laughter. The noise reverberated around the room and made the chandelier tinkle. It sounded like there were ten

149

Granites laughing and when Shane joined it, twenty voices.

Amy scowled. What was so funny?

There was a knock at the door and a rockgoyle came in with a tray of refreshments. She set it down on the table, then backed out of the room.

'Eat and drink, Amethyst. You need something to refresh you,' said Granite. 'Go on, Amethyst, do as I say. Then I'll explain.'

Amy had no appetite. She took a mouthful of water. Granite whispered something to Shane. They both chuckled.

Amy felt so angry she could imagine steam coming out of her ears like in a cartoon. How dare they be so rude? What did they have to whisper about?

'Well!' said Granite, sitting down again. 'Here you are.'

'Yes,' said Amy. 'Here I am.' She dug her hands into her pockets. Her fingers touched Copper's cobweb squares. They were deliciously silky and comforting. Reworked magic. Double strength.

'Are you on your own?'

'Copper and Questrid are at the wolf sanctuary,' she said.

'Good. But they'll come after you, do you think?' croaked Granite. He fixed his black eyes on her. She couldn't look away.

'Not after *me*,' said Amy. 'But they'll come for the cub.'

'Ah, yes, for the cub,' Granite echoed.

Amy pointed at Shane. '*He* took Ralick! Why?'

Granite and Shane Annigan exchanged a smug smile.

'Ralick was our bait, Amethyst.' Granite twisted a large diamond ring round and round on his finger. 'Part of our little plot.'

'What?'

'It wasn't Ralick we wanted, Amethyst,' said Shane. He smirked. 'Sure no, why would we be wanting a wolf-cub? It was Copper—'

'*Copper?*' Amy stared from one to the other. What were they talking about? She couldn't stop looking at Shane Annigan's pearly teeth and glowing face. Suddenly she longed to put him out, like she might put out a lamp, by just clicking a switch.

'Yes,' said Granite. 'We wanted Copper. And you've brought her to us – well, almost. You've done exactly what we wanted.'

'I did?' Amy put her hand on the back of the chair to balance herself. 'How?'

'*How?* Don't you know? By going to Spindle House you made it easier for Shane to get in; they were less suspicious of strangers. You delayed Copper in the Root Room and gave Shane an opportunity to steal the cub. You stopped Cedar from catching Copper by using the one-way tunnel. You spent the night with the pixicles, that gave Shane more time to reach Malachite Mountain …

'Shane could never have kidnapped Copper, but we knew that Copper would come after her cub, so we stole it. You've done well. Very well. Now it's up to us to finish the job—'

Amy felt her mouth drop open. She quickly snapped

151

it shut. They used me! she thought. They manipulated me as if I was nothing, nothing at all.

Something else occurred to her. Something that made her heart sing. They didn't know Ralick could talk! They didn't realise exactly how special he was. They'd missed a trick there!

'Why didn't you tell me the truth?' she said. She sank down onto the chair beside Shane Annigan.

Granite smiled. 'Why should we? We—'

He stopped abruptly. He stared at Shane. Shane's light was suddenly, quickly dimming.

'Shane!'

Shane snatched at his throat, as if he couldn't breathe. He sagged and doubled over. He began to slide off his chair. He made weak, toad-like croaking noises.

'Shane? Are you ill?'

Amy jumped up quickly. She backed away.

'I'm, I'm a little unwell, so I am,' Shane whispered. He took a big breath and straightened up. 'Ah, there, that's better.' His glow returned. 'There must be something here, I'm thinking, something affecting me.' He looked around. 'Sure, I can't think what . . . ' He stared quizzingly at Amy, as if she might know. 'I'll get a rest.' He staggered to his feet. 'Your friends will be here soon and we'll all want to look our best, now, won't we?' He lurched out of the room.

'You've done all that I asked,' said Granite. 'You will be rewarded, never fear. Copper Beech is a rash, headstrong girl. Nothing will keep her from Malachite Mountain . . . and walking straight into my trap!'

***

152

The ugly little female rockgoyle accompanied Amy out, close as a fat shadow.

'Anything else?' The rockgoyle was very close at her elbow. 'I'm here to help.'

'No.'

'Whatever... You're the boss, aren't you?'

Amy spun round. 'How dare you speak to me like that?'

'I can't see you stopping me, Miss Amethyst.'

Amy stared at her. The rockgoyle was smirking. She was!

They were standing in the cavernous hall. The air was cold. Amy tried to think of something cutting to say. As they stood there, a wave of faraway thrumming noises wafted down the corridor towards them.

Amy turned towards it.

The rockgoyle kept her pink piggy eyes focused on the floor. 'Have you been down yet, Miss?'

Amy shivered. She shook her head.

'Come,' said the rockgoyle. When Amy resisted her, the rockgoyle took her firmly by the arm; her claws dug into her skin.

'Listen, I'm sorry I was so bossy to you,' Amy said, suddenly afraid. 'Please let me go. I didn't—'

'Come.'

'But—'

'Come.'

The rockgoyle was much stronger than Amy and there was something inevitable about this journey, Amy thought. I *have* to see what's down there.

The rockgoyle snatched a lantern from the wall. She took Amy through a metal door below the stairs and down a long cold corridor. It wound downwards, deep into the centre of the mountain.

They walked without talking. The only sound was the rockgoyle's flat feet splatting on the stone. Her heavy breathing and sniffling.

As they went deeper underground, the sounds of the rockgoyles grew louder. Thud, thud, pound, went their many feet, with such a dull monotony that Amy knew they were angry and bored. Now she could hear their mutterings and moanings, their pent-up feelings...It made her blood run cold.

Amy tried to stop, but the rockgoyle pulled her on. Amy's mouth was dry. She felt shivery and uncomfortable. She had visions of the horrible faces she'd given some gargoyles; the evil eyes, crooked mouths and scowling expressions. She didn't want to see those faces. She never wanted to see them again. And definitely not alive, down here in the gloom...

The air became wetter, heavier and thicker. The ground was slippery. Icy water dripped and dribbled down the black walls. It was pitch black. The only light came from the rockgoyle's small lantern.

'Have you something to fear?' asked the rockgoyle.

'No,' said Amy. She had never felt so fearful in all her life. 'I'm not a spoiler any more. I'm trying to be nice. I have nothing to fear.' Her heart was racing. Blood pulsed and boiled in her head.

The sound of tramping feet and chanting grew louder.

154

They came to a large room with a high ceiling. Quickly the rockgoyle lit the candles on the wall brackets.

In the centre there was a round, raised pond, full of a green liquid. It was thick and glutinous, like green porridge. It hissed, sucked and whispered as bubbles popped on the surface. The place smelt of mush-rooms. The rockgoyle pushed Amy towards the pond.

Amy couldn't bring herself to look at it. She looked everywhere except at the fizzing green gunge. She tried to cut out the horrible sounds of the rockgoyles. She stared at the walls; they were solid malachite, with streaks and swirls of emerald, turquoise and viridian.

She stared at the massive shuttered window behind which, she guessed, were the rockgoyles. She stared at the very deep, large white sink.

The rockgoyle came and stood next to her.

'Look at the compost.'

'I can't. I don't want to . . . '

She knew now what the rockgoyle planned. She was going to throw Amy in. That was to be her punishment. 'Please, I—'

'It's germinating compost,' said the rockgoyle. She let go of Amy's arm roughly. 'Don't worry, I'm not going to push you in. It's where Granite puts the gargoyles.'

'I remember. Another rockgoyle told me . . . '

'Let me show you.' The rockgoyle took a thing like a shrimping net from a rack on the wall. She plunged it into the bubbling green mess. 'It takes time,' she said, grimly. 'But Granite has time.'

She swept the net backwards and forwards. Bubbles popped and hissed, emitting foul-smelling gases. At last the rockgoyle found what she was looking for. She fished out a grey lump.

Amy recognised it immediately. It was a gargoyle she'd made just before she left Aunt Agnes and Uncle John. It had a long snout like a warthog and bat wings. It was tinged green.

It twitched suddenly.

'It's alive!' Amy squeaked. She jumped back. 'It can't be!'

It was just like the film she'd seen of unborn babies moving in the womb. It wriggled and jerked and made little sucking motions with its mouth.

'Sorry,' she muttered. All this spoiling she was responsible for. 'Really, I am sorry...'

'What are you sorry for?'

'For making them so ugly,' said Amy. 'I thought it was clever. Aunt Agnes was pleased.' She stared at the rockgoyle beseechingly. 'I didn't know...'

'We don't mind being ugly,' said the rockgoyle. 'We are all ugly so we are all beautiful. There is no difference. Though you think to be ugly is to be mean... But we *do* mind being treated like mud. We *do* mind being ordered around. We *do* mind having no name. We *do* mind being made with so much hate. That hatred just fills us with hatred.'

Amy looked down at her feet. 'I really am very sorry.'

'I hope so. Come here, there's one more thing to show you.'

Amy gulped; she wasn't sure she could bear to see any more.

The rockgoyle urged Amy to the window. She threw open the shutters and pulled her up close to look through the dirty glass panes.

'Do you see them?' she whispered.

Amy peered down into an enormous cavern. It was packed with hunched grey figures. An army of ugly, twisted rockgoyles. They were trudging round and round in a slow, monotonous circle. Each rockgoyle so close to the next, that there was hardly an inch between them. They hung their heads. Their clothes were ragged. They chanted a slow, sad song.

'Oh, oh!' said Amy.

'Do you recognise them?'

Amy nodded.

'Granite has done this in just the four months he has been here. They are so mean and nasty that Granite never lets them out. They are truly dangerous. All Granite lets them do is go deep underground to dig. The rest of the time they stay down there in the pits, tramping the rock like animals. You did this, Amy.'

'I didn't.' Amy spun round and stared at the rockgoyle. 'I didn't, not really. It wasn't me. I made clay models the way my aunt told me to. That's all I did. Granite made them alive. The compost made them alive.'

'He is evil, he did give them life, but you are to blame too.'

'I am sorry for making them,' Amy said. 'Truly I am. I didn't know what Granite was doing with my things.'

'You should have found out. You cannot make things and not know what they're for. Where they're going.'

'I know. You're right. I promise I will never, ever, make another horrible object again.'

'Good.'

There was an awkward silence.

'I never asked, but what is your name?' said Amy.

'Primrose.'

'And I'm Amy,' said Amy. 'Not Amethyst...Well, maybe, but not much. Oh, everything's gone wrong at Malachite Mountain for me. Everything.'

'I don't think so,' said the rockgoyle. 'By coming here you have stopped the production of these evil creatures. Enough. I must take you up to your room as Granite ordered.'

Amy sat on the bed. She needed to think. She'd been so horrified by what she'd seen in the deep caverns, she'd let Copper and Ralick slip to the back of her mind.

It's such a mess, she thought. Copper is walking into a trap and it's all my fault...As Amy sat there, gradually the sound of the rockgoyles' faraway chanting and pounding feet crept into her head. It was there all the time, she supposed, but you only heard it when you were quiet and still. So you couldn't be quiet and still. There was no peace here.

'I hate this place!' she said. 'I hate you, Malachite Mountain!'

Something wriggled under her bedcover. Amy pulled back the sheet. The white rat twitched his nose at her.

'You! Why didn't you tell me what Granite and Shane were up to?' she said. 'You could have warned me – even if you do belong to Granite, you could have warned me somehow!'

The rat crawled onto her lap and nudged her fingers with his nose until she stroked him.

'I've been tricked. I hate that Shane Annigan and his cobwebs and everything about him. I hope it was me that made him feel sick. I'd like to put his light out! I feel like going right back, right now— In fact I will. I'll tell Granite just what I think of him and Shane. And then I'll run away.'

She pulled the door, but the door was locked. She was a prisoner.

Amy threw herself back onto the bed. 'It's not fair, it's not fair!' she moaned. Everything always goes wrong for me. She closed her eyes and let the tears dribble down her cheeks. I've done the most terrible things. Those awful monsters down in the caverns. All my fault. *Spoiler. Spoiler.* I so wanted to stop spoiling things . . .

She had a good cry and only stopped when she sensed the white rat creeping around. She felt his tiny claws through her jumper as he climbed onto her chest. Then felt his whiskers tickling her chin.

Amy opened her eyes.

The rat's face was inches from hers. His purple-pink eyes were staring intently into hers.

Clenched between his teeth was Copper's crochet hook.

Amy sat up. The rat tumbled onto the bed, feet in the air. Amy caught him and kissed him.

159

'The hook! Of course I picked it up, didn't I? Copper said she'd used it to pick a lock! Oh, you clever rat.'

Before Amy could try the hook, she heard someone outside the door. She quickly slipped the crochet hook under her pillow.

A rockgoyle came in bringing her blue ice cakes and crystal fizz to drink. It was a different rockgoyle, Amy was sure, from the one that had taken her to the caverns. This one was fatter and its ears were pointed. It had a spiteful-looking mouth.

'I'll run you a bath, shall I? Oh, by the way, Miss ...' The rockgoyle looked round the bathroom door at her. 'Do you know about the mirrors?'

'What?'

'The mirrors. The ones in the bathroom here. Did anyone tell you, they're old and rather wonky? Don't take any heed of them, will you? They distort things.'

Mirrors again. That's what a rockgoyle had said just before Amy left for Spindle House. Amy felt her heart stop.

She remembered the eye-cycle. The image of her own distorted face popped into her head. 'Go away!' she screamed, throwing a pillow at the rockgoyle. 'I mean please, please go away!'

The rockgoyle scuttled across the room and slammed the door shut behind her. The key turned in the lock loudly.

Amy went into the bathroom slowly. She avoided looking at herself in the mirrors which lined the walls. She dived straight into the bath, and lay soaking in the cool foamy water for a long time. She washed her hair. She used every cream and lotion that had been put out for her. She scrubbed her skin till it was red and tingling. Lying in the water she was too low down to see any of her reflection in the mirrors. She was safe for a while.

The white rat sat between the gold taps and washed and combed his fur and whiskers.

Amy got out, still avoiding looking into the wall mirrors. They had steamed up a lot now, anyway. She wrapped herself in towels and went to find some fresh clothes. The rockgoyle had laid out the beautiful soft pale blue cloak on the chest. It was lined with blue and grey mottled fur. Granite had bought it for her. It was what she'd seen herself wearing in the fortune eye-cycle – when she had turned ugly.

Amy kicked the cloak across the room. 'Putting that on would be asking for trouble!' she told the rat. 'I won't touch it.' She chose a long dark red dress instead. It had matching blood-red, leather boots. Their soles were so thin and soft she could feel the hard coldness of the floor through them. She laced them up quickly.

Now she was ready to go. Amy stood very still in the centre of the room.

It was the mirrors that held her there.

You have to know, she told herself. You can't go round suspecting your face is changing all the time. Get in that bathroom, now! She forced herself to turn round, open the bathroom door and go in.

She leaned close to the nearest mirror. She stared at her reflection.

161

'Oh, no!'

Her face was horrible. It was distorted and lopsided. Her eyebrows were thick and shaggy, like twin brown hairy caterpillars crawling over her forehead. Her nose was a swollen, bulbous thing like an old mushroom. She almost couldn't see her eyes, they were such tiny, blood-shot things, devoid of lashes. And her mouth – that was the worst. Her mouth was twisted into a snarl showing long, sharp yellow fangs.

No! No! Amy's eyes filled with tears. The reflection became blurred. Please don't let this be true! Please! Amy ran her fingers all over her face. It felt the same. It didn't feel like it looked. Distorted. The rockgoyle said the mirror was wonky, didn't she? It's the mirror that's wobbly and distorts images, it's not my face chang-ing... Is it?

Amy was shaking. She knew what this meant. The rockgoyle was warning her, was letting Amy see her true self, just as the eye-cycle had. She went back to her room and picked up the rat.

I'm ugly and foul inside and it's showing. I'm turning into the horrid things I made. I'm spoiling myself.

'Why didn't Aunt Agnes let me make nice things, Rat?' she said, stroking him, fiercely. 'If I don't truly change I'll have to stay here forever living like a rockgoyle, with the rockgoyles... I don't want to. I can't.'

She lay back on the bed and closed her eyes. Through the pillow she heard the dull throbbing sound of those faraway chanting voices. It seemed as if her bed trembled in time to the dull thud of pounding hammers and feet striking rhythmically against the rock.

My fault. All my fault, she thought. Those poor miserable things, stuck down there away from the light...

Suddenly Amy felt the rat busying himself about. His little paws trod over her stomach, then up to her face. Something light and warm fell over her cheeks.

'What are you ... ?'

She couldn't speak. All of a sudden she felt so happy. So glad, that she just wanted to hold onto this glorious feeling of bright joy. It was as if she could see inside her own head and the space inside it was enormous. Awhole universe. Or maybe her head had become part of the universe. She buzzed. She glowed. She knew she was smiling. She tried to peer into this great empty space and grasp it. It was such a wonderful, good feeling she wanted to hold it forever.

She couldn't though. Already the sensation was slipping away. Amy put her hands up to her face. She felt a cloth. She opened her eyes. It was the two knitted squares that Copper had made.

'Oh, Rat! It was this!' She pressed the fabric onto her skin. 'You clever thing! It is magic! Like Squitcher said. It's wonderful.'

She closed her eyes again. She couldn't get that wonderful feeling of space back, but she felt different. She felt good. I am not ugly. I am not ugly. Stop me from going ugly, she begged. Stop the rot, please! I'm not going to spoil anything ever again. I'm going to be different! I can do it. Like Wolfgang said, I have a choice. I choose not to spoil.

The rat snuggled under Amy's chin, purring. She lay and watched the sunlight as it moved slowly across the walls, lit up the gold candlesticks and silver ornaments, caught the rich veins in the marble and set it glittering and sparkling. It was very beautiful.

At last she went back to look in the mirror.

The glass was old and tarnished. It was misted with condensation. Amy wiped it quickly with a towel. Her face looked back, her ordinary old Amy face. The glass *was* wonky and wet and that was all.

'Right,' she said to the rat. 'I'm going to do my last bit of spoiling – but good spoiling. I'm going to spoil things for that double-crossing Granite. And horrid Shane. Come on, Rat!'

Getting out of the room was easy. Amy jiggled the crochet hook in the lock and opened the door. The white rat skidded across the polished floor and bumped into the wall beside her.

'Pss, squeak!'

Amy picked him up. 'Rat, dear Rat. Right now, you're the closest thing to a friend I've got,' she told him. 'Let me give you a lift.'

22
The Rescue Party

'I just can't believe it,' said Copper. 'Amy was – she – she was tricking us the whole time?'

Questrid shook his head. 'How mean of her. How mean.'

Wolfgang nodded. 'But she was regretting it.'

'I hope you aren't too jolly squashing-hard on her,' said Squitcher. 'She did write you a sorry-note . . .'

'Yes, I read it,' said Copper. 'And I still say Amy's my friend. She helped us.'

'Did she?' said Questrid coldly. 'Think about it. What did she do? Nothing. She watched us and hung around but she never helped.'

'Oh, you've always been unfriendly to her, Questrid,' said Copper. 'Right from the start.'

'You think everyone's nice,' said Questrid, gently. 'I never trusted her. Remember when I gave her a silver spoon to eat with? It distorted in her hand! She spoiled

165

it. But I never told you because you wouldn't hear a word against her.'

'I wanted a friend,' said Copper, miserably. 'I wanted the Rockers and Woods to be friends.'

'Of course! No blame, Copper,' said Wolfgang. 'To think good thoughts is a fine thing.'

'Granite sent her. He probably sent Shane Annigan,' said Questrid. 'But she didn't know Annigan, did she? Unless she's a brilliant actor. Yet she must have been in on the plot. She kept you in the Root Room longer than you wanted, didn't she, so he could snatch Ralick?'

Copper shook her head. 'I don't think so . . . No, the only bad thing she did was to try to persuade me that you'd taken Ralick.'

'Me?'

'Yes, and worse, I almost believed her!'

They stared at each other.

'Amy brought you here,' Wolfgang said. He sat down. 'Wanted you to come after the wolf cub. So!' He banged his fist on the table. 'So! You must *not* go into Malachite Mountain, Copper!'

'But I have to! If Amy's gone there to get Ralick, then I must too.'

'Wolfgang's right, Copper. Granite's never forgiven you,' said Questrid. 'Copper freed Amber from Granite's clutches. She forced him out of the Rock. She outsmarted him.'

'If he seeks revenge, Copper, that's dangerous,' said Wolfgang. 'Much better you go home.'

166

'Never!' said Copper. 'I'm not going back without Ralick. He's my, my...everything!'

'Wood madness,' laughed Wolfgang. 'Wood shavings for brains. Well, then...I believe the wolf cub is prisoner in the mountain peak.' He paused to pack his pipe and relight it. 'In the Crystal Crown.'

'How do you know, Wolfgang?'

'I have lived inside that mountain,' he said. 'When I was a boy. It was a place for wolves and dwarves. In those days few rockgoyles and not so ugly or mean.'

'Rockgoyles?' said Questrid.

'What's a rockgoyle?' asked Copper.

'What's a...? Think ugly gargoyle with a bit of ogre and you have rockgoyle. They live in the mountains. Are grown there, like mushrooms, in the composting room deep in the mountain. Granite keeps them ugly so they won't leave.'

'OK, OK, enough about rockgoyles. What about this crystal place?' Questrid said. 'Do you know how to get up there, Wolfgang?'

'I do.'

'Then what are we waiting for? The fog's cleared! Let's go!'

Squitcher let out a little squeak. 'Not me, please. I'm sorry, but Boldly Seer is so much puffed-out-exhausted. I must stay and care for her. And I am scared – frightened, it's true. But it's true also we'll need the dragon strong to carry us all home again.'

'Of course you must stay here with Boldly,' said

167

Copper. 'You've been brilliant. Without you we'd never have got here, Squitcher.'

Wolfgang insisted that he come as a guide. The wolves, he assured Questrid and Copper, would be fine without him.

'We'll go round by the waterfall,' Wolfgang told Questrid and Copper. 'Over the hanging bridge and take the path up the back of Malachite Mountain, away from prying eyes.'

Wolfgang led the way. They followed the path Amy had taken (Questrid saw her tracks), then they turned off into the forest. They pushed their way through dense pine trees and leathery-leaved bushes up the mountain-side. When they broke out of the dark woods at last, the sun shone down on them warmly. They blinked in the brilliant light. The snowy slopes around them glistened and twinkled. Now they could see the shape of Malachite Mountain rising up in front of them. It was all sharp crags, black crevasses and smooth green ice. Tiny odd-shaped windows were dotted all over it, glinting brightly.

'Green is the malachite shining through,' Wolfgang said. He pointed to the very top. 'See that? That's the crystal globe!'

Copper squinted up into the sky. The great crystal ball was like a Christmas tree decoration perched on the apex of the mountain. The sunlight bounced off it so it shone like a small sun.

'Poor Ralick,' whispered Copper. 'I hope he's all right.'

They trudged through the snow. Soon Copper heard the trickle of running water. 'That's the waterfall,' said Wolfgang. 'There's a bridge across the gorge. I told you, remember?'

The waterfall was fantastic: half of it was frozen into a massive white-blue frozen wave, like a thick fringe of human hair. It hung way above their heads, suspended over the side of the mountain.

Beneath the cloud of ice, water rushed down the rock. Over the years the running water had cut a deep gorge. Below them the water tumbled and splashed as it made its way down to the valley.

A bridge hung over this gorge.

'We need to cross here,' said Wolfgang. 'The path goes on the other side up to the top of the mountain. No one sees us there.'

Copper stared at the narrow bridge and deep gorge with horror. The bridge was a thin, insubstantial thing made of rope and iron. It looped over the ravine like a bit of string. The wooden planks of the walkway were wet and slimy, constantly sprayed by the waterfall. It did not look safe.

'You first, Copper,' Wolfgang said.

'It looks very rickety,' said Copper.

'It's been there for years. But anyway, you are the lightest and if it breaks, then you are over it and can find the cub. You are most important.'

'That won't break!' said Questrid, laughing.

'I hope you're right,' said Copper.

Gingerly Copper stepped onto the bridge. It swayed

a little. She held on to the rope, letting it slide through her hands as she edged forward. She took five steps and then she was hanging over the ravine. She sensed the great depth below her, it was horrible. Empty. She shivered.

'Don't look down!' shouted Wolfgang.

At her next step, the bridge began to tremble the way a strand of cobweb trembles when a fly is caught on its sticky surface.

'I don't think—'

'Go on! It's fine!' yelled Wolfgang.

Copper went on. The further she got, the more the bridge wobbled and swayed. She was so frightened she closed her eyes. Think of Ralick, she told herself. Think of Ralick. Go on! Go on! You can do it!

She opened her eyes. She began to hurry. She could hear Questrid and Wolfgang shouting encouragement.

The planks were spaced in such a way that her boots caught on them. The ropes beneath her hands were wet and slippery. The whole contraption felt unsafe and wobbly. The other side was looming up. She was nearly there. She ran. She made a flying jump at the end and fell into the deep snow on the far side.

'Done it!'

Her heart was pounding. Blood raced hotly round her limbs. She turned round and waved triumphantly.

'You next, Questrid,' said Wolfgang. 'I follow then behind.'

Questrid jammed his hat down firmly, wrapped his scarf tightly round his neck and set off. He was scared of heights; he felt queasy. He didn't like the way the bridge swayed.

Questrid was halfway across when the wood beneath him dropped with a jolt. He stopped. His fingers curled round the rope rail. He stared down at the wooden planks, willing them to stay still.

A strange whining sound, like a cloud of mosquitoes, filled the air. Something made a popping noise.

Suddenly strands of rope burst out, fraying like bunches of whiskers, all along the length of the bridge. The ropes snapped. The metal rings holding the ropes into the ground clanged and rang as they popped out.

The bridge jolted another stomach-sickening drop. The wooden treads began to shatter, spurting out of their fastenings. They tossed into the air and fell, tumbling into the water below.

'Questrid!' Copper screamed at him.

Wolfgang was shouting. Questrid did not know which way to go. He turned to go back. Wolfgang was sprinting out to help him. He moved and then – there was nothing to run on, his feet were paddling thin air.

The bridge exploded into a thousand shards of wood and rope and iron. Questrid and Wolfgang fell. They hung on to the rope but that snapped. They dropped. They tumbled down and down and disappeared into the black hole below.

Copper screamed. 'Questrid!' Her scream bounced backwards and forwards like an invisible ball round the mountains. She rushed to the edge of the chasm and held onto the remaining post. 'Questrid! Wolfgang!'

171

But there was absolutely no sign of either of them. It was as if they'd never been. There was no movement. The broken rope bridge lay flat against the gleaming sides of the gorge. The only sound was the soft, rushing noise of the water down the rock face.

'Questrid! Wolfgang!'

She called again and again. She could not leave without them. What was she to do? At last, from far, far away, she heard the faintest shout.

'...all right...go on...' It was Questrid.

'Thank goodness. Are you OK?' she yelled back.

OK OK OK, the words echoed around her.

'I'm going on!' she yelled. 'To Ralick!' *Ralick, lick, lick*...

There was nothing more she could do. Thank goodness they were alive. Copper peered into the gorge for one last time, hoping to glimpse her friends. There must be a way out, through the caves or along the river bed, or even up inside the moutain. But she had to leave them to find their own way out.

I'm on my own, now, she thought. She stood up and turned round. She was not alone.

Three pale-skinned, long-haired Rockers stood behind her, grinning.

She was trapped.

23
Saving Ralick

Amy was going up the spiral stairs to the Crystal Crown. She felt sure Ralick would be there. It was the sort of thing Granite would do, lock him up where he could be on show and not easy to rescue. But she was going to save him.

Her feet slap, slapped on the cold, smooth stairs. Her breath clouded in front of her. Every few yards, a foul-faced stone gargoyle leered down at her from the wall. She tried not to look at them.

'It's not my fault,' Amy said to the rat. 'I didn't know. I didn't mean to. I'm sorry.' The gargoyle's eyes seemed to follow her. Blaming her.

She was wondering about Granite too. Why did Granite – *trickster*, *cheat*, *liar* – want Copper? Why?

Amy pushed open the trapdoor to the Crystal Crown very cautiously and went up into the room. The brilliant sunshine bounced back off the white peaks and blinded her. She shielded her eyes, blinked. And when she could see again, she wished she couldn't.

It was awful.

Ralick was dangling from the centre of the glass ceiling on a hook and chain. He was flapping feebly.

He was hanging head down. His back legs were tied together. Amy remembered rabbits hanging outside the butcher's with their heads wrapped in brown paper bags... It looked so unnatural to see him like that. It was all wrong, as if the world was upside down. His legs were red raw from where they'd rubbed against the rope. On the pristine marble floor beneath him were five drops of blood.

Ralick twisted round feebly, half-opened his eyes and growled faintly at Amy.

'Oh, Ralick!' she murmured. She had never felt so ashamed, so sad, so awful.

'I'm sorry! I'm so sorry. Oh, I'm so sorry...' She held out her hand and went towards him. Ralick snapped his teeth at her. She stopped. 'I didn't do it. It's not my fault! Don't blame me! Don't! I would never—'

She waited for him to speak, but he was silent.

'What can I do?' She reached out a trembling hand towards him. 'How can I help?' Ralick growled and snarled and spun on the rope. Two more drops of blood splattered to the floor.

'Maybe the pain has made him mad?' she said to the rat. 'Ralick, Ralick, don't you understand? I want to help!'

'Pss eek pss!' the white rat called. *Snap*, *snip*, *snap*, he flashed his sharp teeth.

'Oh!' She understood. 'You'll bite the rope! Clever thing!'

Amy got as close to Ralick as she dared, then gently put the white rat on the rope. He clung on like an acrobat. Immediately he began to gnaw it.

'I wouldn't hurt you, Ralick,' Amy told the wolf cub, gently. 'I know I *was* going to kidnap you, but that was before I knew. Before I liked Copper. When I thought Granite was good – oh, no, that's not completely true either. I always knew Granite wasn't good.' She stepped nearer, hating the way the wolf cub spun about, knowing how sickening it must feel. 'I just wanted to have something. *Someone.*' She touched Ralick gently, enough to stop the spinning. 'Oh, trust me, Ralick, trust me.'

The rat bit through the last fibre of the rope. Amy reached out to catch Ralick. She half-expected fierce growls and gnashing teeth, but Ralick tumbled into her arms like a dead thing.

Amy had never even held a puppy dog before. The wolf cub was solid and warm and alive. She stroked him, the way she'd seen Copper do. She smoothed the dark hairs which patterned his snout up between his closed eyes. She gently caressed between his ears. She murmured apologies.

'Oh, Ralick, what did they do to you?' She pulled the rope from his sore legs. 'Poor Ralick.'

And she thought she heard a tiny whisper, a growl: 'Thank you.'

Then he lay still.

There was a noise behind her. Shane Annigan burst into the room.

Quick as a flash, the white rat darted up Amy's dress and snuggled down into the safety of the fur lining of her jerkin, squeaking.

'No, no! You won't hurt him!' cried Amy, clutching Ralick to her.

'Ah, now, don't carry on so,' drawled Shane Annigan. He flicked imaginary dust from his jacket and beamed at her. 'I'm just come to tell you that Copper is here, so she is. She wants to see you. We told her how you were after looking to her cub.'

'What?'

'Come on. Come down, do.'

Amy felt suddenly so exhausted she didn't know what to do. Her shoulders sagged. 'I—'

'Come on. Everything is going swimmingly. Let's away.'

Shane held open the trap door. He shivered as Amy passed him, clutching quickly at his heart, as if in sudden pain.

'Are you ill again?' Amy asked him.

'No, sure, I'm dazzling!' Shane laughed. 'Go on, now, you lead the way.'

Granite and Copper were waiting in the Reception Chamber, sitting at the long table. Copper jumped to her feet when she saw Amy and rushed at her. She grabbed Ralick.

'Give him to me!'

Amy sank down on the nearest hard iron chair. Her

arms felt sadly light and empty without the cub. She put her hands on the cool table top and stared at them as if they didn't belong to her. I wish I had never come here, she thought. I wish I'd never left Aunt Agnes and never—

'What have you done to him?' Copper was examining Ralick's bloodied legs. 'Is he all right?'

'Well, well, girls, aren't you friends any more?' Shane grinned. 'Fickle females.'

Granite chuckled. 'Wood and Rock can never mix.' He was rolling a lump of blue rock backwards and forwards over the table as he spoke. 'No alliance there. Never.'

'What about Rock and Air?' asked Copper. 'You two seem very good friends!'

Granite snorted. 'When it suits.'

Amy felt the white rat snuggle against her. He tucked his head into her armpit as if it were a cosy rat hole. You still like me, ignorant, stupid creature, she thought, stroking his back. Dear, silly Rat.

'You've hurt Ralick!' Copper said to Granite. 'You big cowards. You'll pay for this.'

Shane Annigan laughed.

'No, Copper, sure and *you'll* pay for this!' he said.

Copper frowned. 'What do you mean?'

'Isn't it obvious, Copper?' Granite's voice was deep, slow and menacing. 'You must know.'

Copper shook her head. 'I just know two things: One, Amy cheated us—'

'I didn't—' Amy tried to speak, but no one was paying her any attention.

177

'...and two, you bullies have hurt Ralick.'

'But why, eh?' said Granite. 'Why have we gone to all this trouble, eh? Can't you guess? Don't you know what we want...' He paused. 'We want something only you can give us, Copper. You or your mother... We want gold.'

Copper snorted, 'Well that's all right, 'cos I certainly don't have any. I thought you had all the gold there was. Don't you make the rockgoyles dig it out of the mountain for you?'

'I do.' Granite nodded. 'But there's never enough. Never. You can pretend all you like, Copper, but it won't work with us. Shane Annigan has seen you at work in Spindle House. You can make gold! You can knit it out of rock, just like your mother could, and you're going to do it for me.'

'No. Rubbish! I won't! I can't!'

'Won't you...? Really? Think about that very stupid boy you call Questrid. Think about that daft old man with a beard...I have them here, Copper Beech. They were caught by my Rockers in the gorge. Now they are my prisoners.'

'Where...?'

Granite ignored her. 'And, think about it. I can easily take the wolf cub from you again. He's a strong little fellow, isn't he? Able to withstand a great deal of pain, so it seems—'

'Stop it!' Copper tightened her hold round Ralick. She laid her chin on his head. Amy could see her breathing in his scent. 'You're evil, Granite. Truly you are. And wrong! I can't do any magic.' She turned back to Shane

178

Annigan. 'You didn't see me make gold! You didn't see me do anything. You saw the scrap of wood I'd carved, that's all. You didn't see my mother do anything like that either. You lied if you said you did!'

'*She's* lying,' said Shane Annigan, smiling. 'True, I never saw them do it with my own fair eyes, but gold there was, plenty of it. Gold and silver thread. I'd bet my life it was knitted, sure I would. It was so fine and delicate. Where did it come from, if not from her?'

'From the Rock, of course,' said Copper. 'You know it does, Granite,' she added, fiercely. 'Now Ruby is there, she's sending us gold and silver. Every metal one could wish for is being dug out of the Marble Mountains. Woods and Rockers are trading again, like they used to.'

'No, no, that won't do, my little Stick,' chuckled Granite. 'There is too much gold to be accounted for in that way. It's too pure. Too fine. Amber is making it – and so will you.'

'You're wasting your time,' said Copper, shaking her head. 'I wouldn't do it, not even if I could. My mother wouldn't either.'

'Your mother's a very stubborn woman,' said Granite. He ground his teeth. 'You won't be so hard to bend. You're the soft-hearted one, I know it. You and your cuddly little creature with its disgusting mucous membranes slobbering all over the place and its smells and fur, and... You wouldn't want it more hurt, would you? Broken, blinded? Damaged forever? And you're fond of your friends too, I know you are. You all want to go home, don't you? So... Let's show her just what I

179

mean about our prisoners, eh? Think they'll be strung up by now, Shane?'

'Sure they will,' said Shane Annigan, flourishing his magical fingers.

'Where are we going?' said Copper.

'Back to the Crown! Come on!' He yanked her up out of the chair.

'Get off me! Look, I'll do anything, anything,' said Copper. 'But I don't know how to knit gold.'

'Up the stairs,' said Granite. 'Move.'

Granite led the way slowly up the staircase. Amy ran to catch up with Copper. She wanted to snatch a moment so she could explain. As she squeezed past Shane, he stumbled, clutched at his throat and let out a cry of pain.

'What is it?' croaked Granite. He stared back over his crooked shoulder at them.

'Nothing, nothing,' said Shane, sending a searing look at Amy. 'What have you got there, little Rock girl?' he hissed at her. 'What is it? Don't think I won't find it, I will. You can't harm me.'

Amy hardly heard him. Her thoughts were all on Copper. She caught up with her on the next twist of the stairs.

'Copper?'

'Leave me alone,' Copper said. 'After what you did, I just—'

'You must listen. I'm not as bad as it seems, honestly. Ralick knows – I'm on your side.'

'Go away.'

180

'Please . . . I've changed. I got Ralick for you.'

'Thank you for that,' Copper said bluntly. She went on walking. 'Now leave me alone.'

At the last landing they came across two rockgoyles standing guard below the trap door.

'All done as requested,' one said.

Granite nodded. They went up the last few steps. Granite opened the trap door to the Crystal Crown. 'Your friends have been hanging around, waiting to see you,' Granite chuckled. 'Look.'

There were two large caterpillar shapes dangling from the ceiling. Human-shaped sausages. Each one was bound up in a mesh of silvery cobweb.

'Questrid!' Copper cried. 'And Wolfgang! Let them down!'

'Shane's magic thread is a wonderful thing,' said Granite, slowly. 'He's like a poisonous spider, isn't he, our airy friend? He's spun some very unpleasant venom into his thread. It is slowly, slowly eating into their bodies.'

'Oh, no!'

'It's the truth. It's a powerful venom,' said Shane, sweetly. 'Burns the skin. Bites through to the flesh. Eats its way to the bone, sure it does. Agony so it is. Agoneee!' He rubbed his hands together gleefully.

Copper sat down on the bench. She rubbed her eyes. 'Their lives depend on you, Copper, believe me,' said Granite. 'I have this craving for gold. Gold! This urgent desire to feel gold beneath my hands . . .' He rubbed his hands together. 'As soon as I see some, just a few

181

glittering, gleaming strands, I will release your friends. You'll all go free.'

Copper clamped her lips together. She scowled at him. 'You are beneath contempt!' she said coldly. 'I refuse . . . '

'Then I must take Ralick away from you,' said Shane. He strode towards her.

'And they . . . ' Granite nodded towards the ceiling. 'They will die. A shame, but your choice, Copper.'

Copper groaned. 'You beasts! Monsters! I don't have any choice, do I? All right, all right. Give me some needles. I'll try.'

Granite burst into hoarse laughter and slapped her cheerily on the shoulder. 'That's the spirit, girl!'

'Don't touch me!'

'There we are! Sure, and I told you she'd do it,' said Shane. He was gleaming with pleasure. 'The dear little girl that she is.'

'Oh, shut up!' Copper said.

They went down to a lower floor and stopped outside a very big, almost square, metal door. 'This is it,' croaked Granite.

He took a large iron key from his belt and opened the door. This did not reveal a room, but a stone wall. Granite took another key from the cluster at his waist and quickly slipped it into a square hole in the wall – it was not a wall, but a door made of stone. There was a deep, solid-sounding 'clunk' and the door opened very slowly outwards, grinding against the floor.

'Come in, come in.'

182

He led them into a small room, illuminated by only one high, round window. Shane came in, shining. He lit up the veins of red and gold in the walls so they looked like dripping molten metal.

Copper walked over to a big desk in the centre of the room. Amy followed her. The desk was vast. It was made of glossy purple-black marble. On it lay a large chunk of craggy blue rock. Beside that lay a pair of silver knitting needles.

Copper shivered. 'It's madness,' she said, looking from the needles to the rock. 'You can't really think I could make gold.'

'Not *make* it,' Granite corrected her, 'but find it. Coax it out of the rock. You can sense it – a million microscopic molecules – and draw it out. I know you can. Your mother could.'

'But I'm not her!'

'Close enough,' said Shane. 'From what I can see.'

'Oh, this is stupid!' Copper snapped. 'Of course I can't. Anyway, Amber is pure Rock and I'm not. Remember? I'm Copper Beech, half-Wood, half-Rock.'

'I remember,' said Granite, darkly.

Copper put Ralick down on the chair. He opened his eyes briefly, then curled up and slept again.

She put her hand on the lump of rock. Amy watched her. Copper looked up at the three pairs of eyes watching her. 'I'll try,' she said, 'but not with you watching. You have to leave me alone.'

'I don't think—' began Shane.

'She's right,' said Granite. 'It isn't easy. Wasn't easy for Amber. We'll give you time alone. But I warn you, Copper,' he added, glowering at her from beneath his beetle brows, 'your friends don't have much time left.'

Granite pushed Amy out of the room. Shane followed. The heavy stone door slipped into place, then the metal door clanged shut. The key turned loudly in the lock.

Copper was a prisoner.

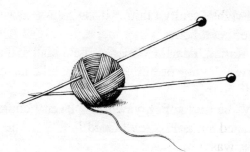

24
What Copper Had to Do

Copper picked up Ralick and felt tenderly all over his body for broken limbs or damage. 'Dear, dear Ralick. Are you all right? Can you hear me? Your poor little legs...'

Ralick lifted his head to Copper's face. He licked her chin.

'I'm worse than I look,' he said, very faintly.

'What do you mean?'

'That was a joke.' He chuckled, weakly. 'I'm good, now I'm with you. Dear Copper.'

She hugged him fiercely. 'They've got Questrid and Wolfgang. They think I can make gold. And Amy's not quite what we thought...'

'What *you* thought. Of course my instincts are sharper than a razor.'

'But I didn't believe you.'

'Amy's not all bad. She set me free.'

'And you're really OK?'

'Never been better.'

'Oh, Ralick, dear!' Copper stroked his head and ears. She kissed the top of his nose. 'Now all I have to do is find gold in this.'

'Easy,' he said softly, yawning. 'Even I could do it.'

'I must think gold. Gold. Gold!'

'Except—'

'What?'

'If you find it, if you *can* do it, you'll never get free. Granite'll never let you go. He'll lock you up, like he did Amber. You'll never see Spindle House again...'

'Perhaps...' said Copper. 'But if I don't, Questrid and Wolfgang will die. So might you. I have no choice...'

Copper closed her eyes and pressed her palms either side of the chunk of cold rock.

She tried to picture the millions of particles of gold inside, the way Granite had described it. First, it was like picturing the sky, studded with brilliant diamond stars. The stars gradually diminished into the tiniest pinpricks of golden light. Then, behind her eyelids, the particles began to whirl and whizz around, as if stirred by an invisible, giant spoon. The dots crashed against each other, coalescing, sticking together into long strands of shimmering beads...The rock was hot. Her hands were hot. Her heart raced. Suddenly she felt a gushing river of hot yellowness streaming through her fingers. Her eyes flew open: 'Oh, no!'

'I suppose that means you thought some,' said Ralick. Copper nodded.

Ralick's ears went down sadly. 'Hidden talents, Copper...'

Copper picked up the knitting needles and poked the end of the left one experimentally into the rock. Immediately, a strand of gold slithered out. It was like a long skinny metallic worm. It wrapped itself round her needle. Her right needle did the same. More and more gold came spilling out of the rock. She knitted it so quickly, sparks flew.

'Oh, my golly, Ralick, look! It's magic...'

The gold thread looped itself round the needles. The needles clacked and clicked against each other. The thread knitted itself into a delicate fabric in a beautiful, complicated stitch she'd never seen before. Soon she'd knitted a large square of gold. It lay on the desk, like a gleaming piece of finest gold leaf.

'Stop now,' said Ralick quietly.

Copper went on knitting.

'Stop now.'

'Look at it! Look at it, Ralick, I can do it! I can make gold. We'll be rich! We'll take it all back to Spindle House and we'll be so rich. We can have everything we want—'

'Stop!' Ralick caught the end of the needle in his teeth and tugged. It clattered to the floor, breaking off a long strand of gold thread. The gold thread lay across the desk like a long, thick, golden hair.

Copper stopped, hands held mid-air, breathing hard.

'Yuck!' she said at last. She dropped the other needle. She wiped her hands down her trousers as if they were contaminated. 'Thanks, Ralick. That wasn't nice. You'd think it would feel good to make gold, but it's awful.' She shook her head and licked her lips, trying to dispel the taste, the sensation of it. 'I feel as if I've eaten metal,' she said. 'I smell. Like I've held a thousand pennies in my hot, sweaty hands. Ugh, I'm dirty. I'm—'

'Shh! What's that?'

There was a sudden rasping noise; someone was trying to unlock the outer door.

'Them already?' she jumped up in alarm. 'No!'

The metal door swung open with a whine and a groan. Through it they heard Amy's muffled voice.

'It's me, can you hear me? Copper?'

'Phew – it's only her. Yes. I can hear you.'

'I came back! I opened the door with your crochet hook, Copper,' said Amy. 'But the other door, the stone one, how do I get through that?'

'Are you sure you want to?' said Copper.

'Oh, Copper, don't hate me, don't,' said Amy. 'I'm not all bad, honestly. Let me explain...I've come to help – only I can't open this stone door.'

'She sounds as if she means it,' whispered Copper.

Ralick nodded. 'We've nothing – except this prison – to lose.'

'He had a small stone key,' said Copper. 'I wasn't really watching, but it looked like a sort of square, with holes in it on the end of a stick – like a square lolly.'

Copper and Ralick could hear Amy's hands flickering over the door, as if a group of mice were scampering over it. She was searching for the right gap in the stone blocks.

'Found the place, but of course no key.'

25
Escape

'I'll be back!' Amy called out. She ran to her room. 'Don't worry!'

The white rat was inside her jerkin. She put her hand over him so he wouldn't fall out. 'All right, Rat? Got to get a key. A key for stone.'

She had a plan. She still had the tool set her Uncle John had given her. It was in her room. She could make a key with those tools. But she needed something to make a key out of... metal would take too long. A soft stone would be perfect... There! A small stone statue of a woman carrying a large fish. Her arms were raised above her head as if she were showing the fish to someone. 'That'll do, Rat,' said Amy. 'The fish is just about the size of that hole.'

'Eek, psss.'

'And it's soft, easy to carve... Let's go.'

She scuttled back to Copper's prison.

The keyhole looked square-shaped on the outside, but when she pushed her fingers into it, she found indentations and hollows on the inside. It was a complicated lock.

'We have to get Copper out of there. Here goes, Rat.' Amy started filing the stone figure to make the key shape. She kept alert for approaching footsteps. She dug and chiselled and cut it.

'Nearly there, Copper. Almost done.'

The rat helped too. He put his nose and whiskers into the keyhole to see more clearly what it was like inside. Then he backed out, squeaking and nodding excitedly, pointing with his nose at where Amy was to make changes to the key.

'Oh, *in* there and out *there*? I see!' Amy said. She honed the stone key. She rubbed and smoothed it until the lollipop shape was covered in zigzag lines and hollows. Finally when she had ground down a sharp corner on the key, it felt right.

'Done it!' She turned the key in the lock. There was the sound of levers tumbling and falling. A mechanism whirring. When she heaved on the heavy door, it swung open.

Amy ran into the room. 'We did it . . . Oh, whoah!'

The gold knitting lay gleaming on the desk like a pool of golden syrup.

'Copper! You've made it! Fantastic! Gold! You can do it!'

'No.'

'But Copper, you can!' Amy pulled the doors closed

behind her, enough to block out their voices, but not enough for the locks to click shut. 'You'll be rich. Gold out of rock. Whenever you want. All day long. Your world has just changed. This is fantastic!'

Copper shivered. 'I don't want it to change. I hate the stuff, Amy, I hate it! My mum didn't want the gift of knitting gold and nor do I. That's why she hid my needles, I understand now... If Granite sees this I'll be a prisoner like she was, knitting gold, hour after hour after hour. Amy, if you're my friend, help me!'

Amy took a deep breath. 'I am your friend. But, well, I'm truly impressed. Such stuff!' She picked up the gold knitting. It was like the fragments Copper had knitted from Shane's cobweb thread. It was silky, floating and delicate. She tugged it between her hands. 'It's strong as iron!'

'Will you just forget about the gold,' said Copper. 'Let's go.'

'Yes, but listen,' said Amy, grabbing Copper's arm. 'I thought of something. They want you. So if you were wearing my clothes and I was wearing yours, you'd stand a better chance of escape.'

Copper looked doubtful.

'Listen. Listen. I'm sorry I helped Granite,' said Amy. 'I can see you don't trust me. But, truly, I don't want to spoil everything, Copper, and only be known for that. Believe me. Everyone always told me how horrible the Wood Clan people are and that's what I wanted to believe. But you're not. You're just like us Rockers, only different.'

'Of course we are.'

'I trust her, Copper,' said Ralick. 'She means well. She wants to put things right.'

'I do, Ralick. I do.'

'I do trust you,' said Copper. 'Of course I do, Amy. I've always liked you, I promise. OK. Let's do it.'

Copper laced herself up in Amy's red boots and dress. She hid her tell-tale coppery hair under Amy's red hat. Amy put on Copper's jumper and trousers. Immediately she felt hot and uncomfy. She fastened the toolkit around her waist and pulled her jumper over it. She put on Copper's coat and hat. Now she felt hot enough to explode.

'Brrr. I'm freezing. Thanks, Amy,' said Copper. 'I don't know how I'll get out of here, but I will. I'll go straight to Squitcher. He'll help.' She glanced back at the gold fabric. 'What about that?'

'I'll hide it down my boot,' said Amy. She squished it down inside Copper's fur-lined boot. 'We don't want Granite to see it. If they catch me they'll soon see it's me. They'll think if you did make gold that you took it with you, won't they?'

Copper grinned. 'Good thinking.' She picked up Ralick and made for the door. Footsteps were approaching. 'They're here!'

Copper and Amy looked around for a way out. There was none.

The last strand of gold on the desk.

'They'll see it!'

Amy lunged for it and grabbed it at exactly the same

instant as Copper. They found themselves holding it taut between them.

Without a word, but silently visualising the same picture, they knelt either side of the door. They hid back against the wall and held the gold thread stretched out across the doorway like a tripwire.

They saw Shane's light first, seeping out ahead of him. They felt the heavy, grainy presence of Granite nearby.

'She's escaped!' Granite yanked the door open. Shane was right behind him.

Neither saw the gold thread in their path.

Granite charged in. He tripped. He fell headfirst into the room, slapping down hard onto the marble floor. Shane toppled over him. They were a tangle of arms and legs. Copper had the chance she needed. She grinned triumphantly at Amy. She picked up Ralick, jumped over the prostrate bodies and was gone.

Amy hesitated. It had been that kind, happy look from Copper that had delayed her. They were friends...

Amy got to her feet. She tried to get past Granite. Granite grabbed her foot and pulled her over. She crashed down hard on the floor.

'Not so fast, Miss Beech,' Granite hissed. He got up, holding onto her boot all the while. 'You're not going anywhere.'

Amy kicked him off. She shoved at him with her foot. She struggled, but Shane was on his feet too and grabbed her. He stared into her face.

'It's *her*!' cried Shane. 'The Rock one, so it is!' He backed away. 'The girls have tricked us.'

193

Granite was standing up, too. He pulled Amy's beret off and revealed her thick black hair.

'Traitor!' he croaked. 'Traitor. Double-dealing traitor. You'll pay for this. We must get after that Stick—' He broke off. He sniffed. '*Gold!*' He peered round the room.

Taking Amy with him, he began to inch, toad-like, round the room. 'Where is it? I smell it, I smell it. She made gold, didn't she?' He swept his fingers across the desk and held them up to the light, examining them for specks of gold dust. 'I knew she could and she did. She's taken it back to her Wood friends, has she?'

He pushed Amy into the corner, and sat down on the chair.

'I don't know,' said Amy.

'Didn't you want the gold? Didn't you want all the fine things I had to offer? Stupid Amethyst, have you no sense?'

'I, I . . .'

'What a hopeless girl you are. What will become of you now, hmmm? Will Agate and Jarosite want you back? Will I cast you out into the snow? Well, you will not remain my guest in Malachite Mountain for one minute longer, that is for certain. Call yourself a Rock? Huh! I do not want to look on your miserable traitor's face, ever again.'

The two men were staring at her with such loathing. Tears welled up in her eyes.

'In fact,' croaked Granite, 'since I can assure you that neither Agate, Jarosite or I ever want to see you again, you can stay here. Locked in this place for the rest of your miserable life.'

194

'No. You couldn't!'

'I certainly could. And I will. What do you say, Shane?'

'It's a fine idea,' said Shane Annigan, grinning. 'Sure it is. I like the idea – she's dangerous. Let her die here. Alone.'

'You can't!' Amy ran at the door, but Shane got there first and pushed her back. She tumbled against the desk, bruising her hip.

'You can't!'

Granite laughed. 'Goodbye.'

The great stone door closed behind them.

'Sure and it was never a pleasure knowing *you*!' cried Shane.

'No keyhole on that side, Amethyst!' Granite shouted back. 'No way out at all – unless you jump!'

Amy ran back to the door but there was no door handle, no lock, nothing. She put her ear against it, there wasn't a sound. She was trapped.

26
On Ice

Amy leaned against the cold stone wall. She stared at the room's dark walls. Her eyes followed the blood-red veins and purple swirls. Was she going to stare at them for the rest of her life? Was this the end? She felt her heartbeat quicken. She was panicking. That was no good. She had to keep calm. At least she had the rat with her. He'd keep her company.

She looked around the room again. There was a window. That was her only chance.

She shrugged off the coat and thick jumper. She dragged the big chair over and climbed on it. She could reach the window now. It was a circle of blue glass, about the size of a bathroom sink, set into the thick wall.

Amy leant on the sill and looked out. The window was halfway up the mountainside and all she could see was sky.

196

Her chest went tight. Her heart stopped beating. She was doomed.

'That doesn't look very hopeful, does it, Rat?' She whispered. 'I suppose I might wait for Copper to come back... But she might never come back. I can't just sit here, can I?'

'*You just sit there and wait until you're spoken to.*' Aunt Agnes's much repeated words whined in her head.

'Not this time, Aunt Agnes. Leave me alone.'

The rat twiddled his whiskers. He wiped his little paws across his face.

'I have to get out,'Amy said to it. 'Maybe Copper will need me... No time to waste... so... I think I'd rather fall all the way down the mountain and die than sit in here and die.'

There was no way of opening the window. She picked up the rock from the desk and threw it at the glass with all her might.

The window shattered. Glass tinkled onto the marble floor. More glass went flying out of the window. Amy heard it splintering and chiming as it hit the rock below.

'*Who's going to clean that up? You're such a messy girl, you always have been...*'

'Please leave me alone, Aunt Agnes.'

Quickly Amy climbed back onto the chair. She wrapped her hand in the coat and punched out the remaining shards of glass. When it was clear she climbed up onto the deep sill and stuck her head out into the fresh, sharp air.

Down, up, sideways, it was all the same. Sheer ice.

197

Above her, below her, the cloudy green ice of Malachite Mountain stretched out like glass.

Amy slipped back inside. She took a big breath.

'Rat, it's the only way to go. We have to do it. Are you ready?'

'*You're scared of heights, you know you are. Don't try this, you hopeless girl . . .*'

'Be quiet!'

The rat dived under her shirt, claws scratching against her skin and curled itself into a ball.

'Sorry, Rat, I didn't mean you be quiet. But anyway, I'll take that as a yes.'

Amy hoisted herself onto the windowsill. She stuck her head and arms out through the window. Below her, the mountain slipped away, down, down, down. It seemed to go on for miles and miles. Above her it reached into the sky. The dome of the Crystal Crown glinted on the peak.

'Up or down?' she asked the rat.

The white rat poked its nose out between the shirt buttons, sniffing the air. 'Pss, pss.'

'I agree, I rather think it's going to be down,' said Amy.

The rat's beady bright eyes scanned up and down across the mountainside. His whiskers flickered. His pink nose twitched and wrinkled as if he was thinking. Finally, with a positive sort of 'squee-ak' the rat suddenly leaped off the windowsill and launched himself into the air.

'Rat!' Oh, my goodness. He'll die, thought Amy. He'll fall to his death. 'Rat!'

But the white rat didn't fall. He had leapt sideways, about an arm's-length from the window. He pressed himself flat, holding onto the ice by his claws. He lay so flat against the ice, he looked like a white handkerchief knotted at four corners.

'You silly thing!' cried Amy. She leaned out to try and reach him. 'You nit! Now what? I can't reach you!'

The rat was not worried. His nose was twitching. His eyes darted everywhere. He grinned at her.

Then he released his grip on the ice. Just a tiny bit, until only the end of a claw held him. He began to slide slowly down the mountain. His nails squealed against the ice like chalk on a blackboard, as he went.

'Oh, you clever rat!' cried Amy. 'I see it. I understand!'

She opened her tool apron. She chose a small pick and a chisel. Holding one in each hand, she turned herself round and slipped herself feet first out of the window. 'Oh, golly, Rat! This is so awful!'

'Squeak, squeak,' called the rat. It really did sound encouraging.

Amy's legs were now dangling out of the window. She was holding on to the windowsill by the ends of her fingertips. She didn't want to let go. She kept thinking about that great drop below. She imagined herself falling, slipping and slithering all the way to the bottom . . .

'Squeak. Pss. Eeek!'

'Yes,' said Amy. 'I'm coming.' She moved one hand out and dug the pick into the ice. When she had all her weight on that, she moved her other hand out. She dug in the chisel until it would take her weight. She hung there.

'Oh, my goodness!'

It was so terrible. She pictured herself, like a fly, a dot on the great white vastness of the mountain. 'Oh, my, my, my...'

She couldn't move.

She took a big breath of the sharp air but it didn't help. It was too much for her. She was stuck.

'Oh,' she said in a small voice. 'Oh, I'm stuck. Rat, I'm stuck here, hanging like a spider or something... Rat!'

It's all gone wrong, everything, again. My plan to save Copper hasn't worked. She's probably right now being locked in a dungeon. Here I am, stuck on the mountain, about to fall to my death...

'*Yes, silly girl, stupid girl, you spoil everything, don't you?*' Aunt Agnes was a mosquito whine in her head.

'Leave me alone, Aunt Agnes, please. Please.'

Amy's arms were on fire. Her fingers were wrapped so tightly round the metal tools she didn't think she'd ever be able to unbend them. They were beginning to burn and cramp.

She closed her eyes and rested her cheek against the ice. 'I can't, I can't, I can't... Aunt Agnes is right. She knows me and I'm useless... I'm doomed.'

But the rat came back.

He inched himself across the ice, hanging on by the tips of his tiny claws. He crawled across the smooth surface until he was close to Amy's face.

'I can't,' whispered Amy. 'Help me.'

'Pss, pss, squeak.' The rat moved up to the steel pick in her right hand. He pushed his nose beneath it. Immediately, the tiny pick lifted a fraction out of the ice and grazed over the ice. Amy slipped. She screamed. But as soon as she slipped and screamed, she thrust the pick back into the ice...only now it was twenty centimetres lower down and all her weight was on her left arm.

Her heart was pounding hard in her chest, she could feel it beating against the mountainside. 'All right, all right.' She breathed slowly. 'I understand. Yes.'

Amy dug the pick in again very hard. Now, very carefully she released the chisel, which was easier to get out than the pick because it wasn't curved. It would be harder to get in, too. She let it slip a little way, then the moment she felt the speed increasing too quickly and her right hand take too much of her weight, she thrust the chisel back into the ice. Both arms were now taking her weight.

'Eeek eek!' said the white rat chirpily. He set off, skating and slip-sliding downwards and sidewards. He looked as if he'd done it all his life.

Amy watched him.

Her stomach tightened when she saw below her the miles and miles of mountainside. Slippery green rock, sheer ice and snow and ledges...ledges! Yes, there were bumps and cracks and wasn't that a window? It would be a window, of course it would. Her spirits soared.

'See, Aunt Agnes, you're wrong. I can do this!'

Amy let go with the pick again and moved slowly

201

down the mountain. It was hard. Her shoulders screamed out in agony. She imagined her bones popping out of their sockets under the strain, her tendons and sinews snapping like wires in an electric cable and bursting apart. Every-thing hurt. But as she grew more confident, she found invisible protrusions and tiny jutting bits where, by kicking her legs into the ice, she could rest for a second.

Looking down, she saw the rat had almost reached a window. Slowly, Amy inched her way sideways and down towards him. 'I'm coming. I'm coming!'

She was over confident. She made one hurried move and the pick didn't connect; it slipped, gouging a long deep channel in the ice. She was pulled up tight with a terrible wrench. All her weight hung on the chisel.

'Ow! Help!'

She swung, legs scrabbling for a hold, her right arm jabbing the pick at the ice. At last she got a hold. Her feet found substance to stand on; she stopped falling. A hot tear ran down her cheek. 'Oh, Rat, Rat,' she muttered. 'This is the worst bit of my entire life.'

She took a deep breath. From now on, every move, until she reached the window, was going to be slow and careful. She inched in crab-like manoeuvres across the ice until at last she reached the rat. He was sitting on a wide windowsill, licking his paws. Amy guessed they were cold and sore.

'Done it.' Amy slithered onto the sill beside him. She tightened her fingers around the window frame. It felt good and solid.

202

Through the window she spied an empty room. Good. But even if it had been full of rockgoyles, Granite and Shane, she still would have gone in. She had no choice.

Amy pushed hard against the window frame and it burst open. She tumbled onto the floor. 'Phew!' She sat on the solid ground, relishing the feel of it. Her hands were trembling, her legs were shivering from the effort. She was panting and hot. Her borrowed trousers had ripped at both knees, her shirt was wet and torn.

The rat jumped down beside her.

'Did it,' said Amy. She stroked his head. 'Thanks Rat.'

The rat smiled his rattish smile and scampered up her arm. He snuggled under her chin. He nudged her with his cold nose.

'Thank you,' Amy said again. Her legs were still shaky. Her fingers felt cramped and stiff. She put away her tools in the apron and stood up. 'Now, I suppose I'd better get a move on.'

Outside the room, she made a discovery: she was on the same landing as her bedroom. She could get fresh clothes.

She ran to her bedroom and pushed open the door. Then her heart stopped with a jolt.

She, *Amy*, was already there! She was standing at the end of her bed. She was wearing the blue, hooded cloak that Granite had given her.

It wasn't possible!

The eye-cycle! It's what I saw in Squitcher's eye-cycle, she thought. My fortune. But how can I be there?

Very slowly, the figure turned round. It wasn't Amy.
It was an ugly, grey-skinned rockgoyle with a hairy chin
and pointed ears. The rockgoyle grinned sheepishly at
Amy.

'Thought you'd gone,' she muttered. 'They said you
weren't coming back.' She shrugged off the cloak. 'Just
trying it on.'

'Have it, have it,' said Amy. She rushed at her and
thrust the cloak back over the rockgoyle's shoulders. 'It
suits you. Honestly. It looks so much better on you.
Please take it.'

'Sure? Don't need to tell me more than once. Thanks!'
The rockgoyle pulled it round her and ran out of the
room.

Amy twirled round in delight. She made the rat so
dizzy, he crawled out and jumped onto the bed, shaking
his head.

'It wasn't me in the eye-cycle!' she cried. 'Not me!
Not my face!'

She dashed into the bathroom and stared at her
reflection. It was exactly as it should be. Her nose was
the same, her big blue eyes were the same. Her chin,
cheeks and brows all normal. 'I'm not turning into a
rockgoyle! I'm not! I'm not!'

'Eeek,' said the rat.

'Yes, eeek! Isn't it great? I feel so much better. I'm
not spoiling, Rat. I'm not ugly and I can make things
good.'

Amy ripped off Copper's clothes and put on her own.
She chose boring old things she'd brought with her from

204

the South. She held Copper's shirt against her nose for a second before casting it off. It smelled of wood shavings, sawdust and something cosy and pleasant that she couldn't identify.

'First I thought that was so disgusting,' she told the rat. 'Now I sort of wish I smelled like that, but I don't. That's sweet little Copper and I'm hard little Amy. But I can be kind, reliable Amy too.'

'Eek, eek,' said the rat.

Amy took the gold square from inside her boot. It was exquisite. She could dribble it through her fingers like liquid, but it was as strong as Shane's cobweb thread. She put it into her left pocket. In her right were the cobweb squares.

'Double magic,' she told the rat. 'For spoiling everything for Granite and Shane Annigan if I can.' The white rat wiggled his whiskers at her and squeaked in agreement. 'Absolutely,' Amy said. 'This isn't over yet! To the Crystal Crown!'

27
Amy Spoils Things for Shane Annigan

Amy ran up the narrow spiral staircase to the Crystal Crown. The trap door was open and she crept through warily. The startling brilliance of the sun stopped her momentarily. She halted, blinking.

Questrid and Wolfgang twirled sadly from the ceiling, like old Christmas decorations or dried old hams. Shane Annigan and Granite were there too. They had their backs to her and had not seen her. Still, she knew there was no chance of her getting the prisoners down.

Had Copper escaped?

There was something high up above them in the sky. Granite and Shane were watching it. It suddenly came swooping over the Crystal Crown, a flash of pink and purple and silver.

Boldly Seer! It was the dragon.

She skimmed past, then came back and hovered like a

glimmering silvery bird. The fine pink skin was stretched tight between the webs of cartilage so her wings were like a giant kite.

Amy's heart skipped a beat. Something inside her soared upwards towards the dragon, willing it success. Go, go! she urged it silently. Go on, you beauty!

Then she saw that Copper and little Squitcher were on the dragon's back.

Copper had got free!

I did that, Amy told herself. I got her out. There's something I haven't spoiled. She grinned happily.

'Dragons?' Granite said.

'Just one dragon,' said Shane Annigan.

Granite waved a fist towards it. He stamped his foot. 'Is that her up there? Is that the Beech Twig? Shoot that flying lizard out of the skies!'

Amy didn't think either of the two men had a weapon, she couldn't see one. Still, if they were going to try and shoot Copper down, she'd stop them. She crept up behind them.

As she got nearer, Shane reached for his throat. He made a choking sound and spun round.

'You!' he spat at her. His face went hard and sharp. 'Sure, it's her again, Granite. Your Rock girl has escaped!' He sneered at her.

Granite growled. 'How? How did you get out? Do you know some magic I don't?' He ground his fist into his palm as if he was trying to wear his hand away. 'I am angry. I am very angry. No time now. We'll deal with her later.' He glared up at the dragon again.

Shane retreated. Amy saw his light glowed again with renewed strength when he moved away from her.

That happened before, she thought. Did I do that? Could I have something that did that?

The knitting.

She clamped her hand over the pockets containing the squares. That was it! Squitcher said they were strong. They'd made her feel better but they made Shane feel bad. A taste of his own medicine. Ha!

The Questrid-shaped bundle wriggled and whined. Amy shivered. Poor thing! Shane said poison would be eating at their flesh. Were they in terrible pain? Was the poison working right now?

She cupped the white rat in her hands, kissed his head. 'Go on,' she whispered. 'You can do it. Just like you did for Ralick. Go!'

She threw the rat onto the swinging cocoon.

'Hey!' said Granite. He jerked round. 'Is that my rat? Blast you, Rat! Where've you been?'

The rat ignored him. He raced up to the top of the cocoon. He bit at the thin cord. He chewed and nibbled and gnawed, but Shane's evil cobweb thread was too strong for him. He couldn't cut it.

Shane watched the rat. He smiled. He licked his pearly teeth with his tongue. 'Now and what sort of nasty little creature would that be?' he said. 'Seems it's changed sides, Granite. It happens. Sure, it's a nasty, dirty, spoiling thing, so it is.'

Shane took a smooth stone from his pocket. He rolled it in his fingers, as if admiring it. Suddenly he took aim.

Amy realised what he was going to do.

'Don't!' she yelled. She leaped towards him.

Shane threw the pebble. It whizzed through the air. It hit the white rat squarely and sharply on his head.

The rat went still. A look of total, bemused surprise filled his eyes. Slowly, very slowly, he looked round the room, searching for Amy. He found her. Their eyes locked. He opened his mouth and gave the smallest squeak. 'Oh, Rat!' Amy cried.

The rat's eyes, so full of sparkle a second before, blanked and went glassy. Before Amy could reach him, he fell backwards and toppled onto the floor.

'Ahhh! You've killed him!' Amy scooped the rat up. He was warm and limp. His tail lay across her wrist as lifeless as a strand of string. A tiny drop of blood coloured his perfect shell-pink nose. 'Oh, Rat, my dear Rat.'

'Killed, is it? Well, and am I surprised, d'you suppose? Wasn't that just what I was aiming to do?' Shane Annigan grinned at her. 'I'll have no interference from rodent beasties and girls the likes of you!'

'I hate you. He was my friend. You pig! I—'

Suddenly a great whirling orange and red balloon of flame came hurtling out of the sky towards them. It hit the Crystal Crown with an ear-splitting crack.

'Dragon fireballs!' Shane Annigan yelled. He ducked behind Granite.

Amy heard a creaking noise, like ice cracking underfoot, as a criss-crossing, zigzagging line careered across the glass. The dome was cracking. Amy covered her head with her hands and peeped up.

The sky was blotted out by Boldly Seer's pale underbelly and vast wings. She hovered above them. She sent more fireballs crashing and sparking over the glass. Gusts of purple smoke and showers of ashes rained down on them.

Suddenly the dragon swerved up, away. For one awful moment Amy thought that she was leaving, then she turned and flew back towards them. This time she approached the dome with her scaly legs extended, claws fanned out.

'What's it doing? Stop them, Shane!' Granite said. 'Do something!'

Boldly Seer landed on the top of the crystal. Her weight squashed the dome as if it were a rubber ball and its sides bulged. Minuscule cracks shot over it, covering every inch. Splinters tinkled to the floor.

The dragon rested on the apex for only a second while she grasped the top of the dome in her claws. She beat her wings strongly. She began to pull. The top of the dome came off. The two suspended bodies were still attached below. The dragon lifted it all.

Fantastic! Amy thought. As if it was a jampot lid, nothing but a jampot lid! 'Go on, go on!' she yelled. 'Go!'

The walls of the dome collapsed in splinters around them.

The crystal was heavy. There were all the fine metal struts that made the dome as well as the glass, metal hooks and the bodies. Boldly Seer struggled. She flapped her wings hard. She snorted and puffed, trying to get away with her trophy.

210

'Go, go!' Amy urged her.

'Be quiet!' Shane snapped at her. He was as pale as marble. His eyes harder than diamonds.

Shane shot out his arm. He pointed up at Boldly Seer. A silvery thread flew from Shane's fingers towards the dragon. It looked like a silver spear, or a shining needle as it streamed to her.

Zap! It hit Boldly Seer with a metallic sound. Immediately it wrapped itself around her leg, coiling round and round. The dragon jolted, arrested in mid-flight. She couldn't see what had happened. She thrashed her wings, trying to rise, straining against the anchor that held her. But she couldn't move.

She screamed. It was awful.

'No, no. Poor Boldly. Don't,' begged Amy.

'That dragon's nothing but a scallywag, sure it's not,' Shane said lightly. He put both hands on the silvery line. Slowly, slowly, like a fisherman fishing the skies, he began to haul the dragon in. 'Don't they know there's no messing with Shane Annigan, the man of the air? Don't they? Dragon Destroyer. Copper Capturer!' He laughed. 'Sure!' he called up at them, 'And it's the air is my element and these strands are stronger than gold. I have you now. You'll never get away!'

Amy had seen and heard enough.

She leaped at Shane. She wrapped her arms round his neck and dragged on him with all her weight. 'Stop it! Stop it!'

'Don't bother,' drawled Granite. 'Nothing brings down the man of the air – not even me.'

But he was wrong.

The moment Amy touched him, Shane jerked. He might have been struck by an electric current. His knees buckled and he collapsed.

'Get off me! Get her away, Granite!' He threw Amy aside. He crawled across the floor, keeping hold of the silver thread. He dragged himself to his feet to face her, holding out his arms to stop her. Amy ran at him again.

'I hate you!' she yelled.

She jumped at him. She had the two cobweb fabric pieces in her hands. She slapped them against his cheeks. She rubbed them all over his skin.

'There!' She pushed them through his pale hair. 'There!' His ears. 'Take that!' And eyes. 'There!'

Shane screamed. He tottered as if his legs had snapped. He spun round, he fell. He crashed down amongst the broken glass.

The cobweb thread snapped with a loud *twang*.

Boldly Seer rose up like a newly-inflated balloon. Her wings pushed against the sky, she went higher and higher, carrying her passengers to safety. She flew and flew until she was soon no more than a dark dot in the blue sky.

It was suddenly very quiet. Fresh, icy mountain air swept around them now the walls of the Crystal Crown had crashed down.

'Pleased with yourself?' asked Granite. He was slumped on the bench. The wind lifted his rat's tails of grey hair and whipped them around his face.

Amy picked up the white rat and cradled him. She

212

kissed and kissed the little flat bit between his ears. She had nothing to say.

Shane startled them both by letting out a strange, long groan. It was followed by an ear-piercing, high-pitched whistle. It sounded like a kettle boiling a long way off.

'I didn't mean to,' said Amy, glancing at him. 'I just wanted to stop him.'

'You've done that, I would say,' said Granite, grimly. 'More than I could do. The Will-o'-the-Wisps are a dangerous, shifty lot.'

'But wasn't he your friend?'

Granite shook his head. 'I have no friends.'

Another terrible whistle screamed from Shane Annigan's half-open mouth. This time it was accompanied by a sort of long sigh, like air escaping from a punctured tyre.

Shane was deflating.

His face lost substance, the way people's faces do who've been ill for a very long time. But this happened in five minutes, not months. His hands withered until they looked like empty white gloves sticking out of his sleeves. His chest sank, his legs and arms went flat. His skull lay like silk on the ground. He was nothing, just a shell, like a skin wearing empty clothes. A wisp of cloudy air floated from his lips. Then nothing.

'I'm sorry, but I'm not sorry,' said Amy. She stroked Rat. 'I'm glad too. It's the best bit of spoiling I've ever done. He killed my rat. He was nasty.'

'You've done me a favour, though I don't suppose you want to hear that,' chuckled Granite. 'Shane bullied

213

me into this. He wanted half my gold for his help. I wouldn't have shared it with him, anyway. Not for nothing.'

'Gold? Always it's gold. Here, for you!' Amy threw Copper's knitted gold square at Granite. It sailed through the air as if it was a globule of syrup.

Granite snatched the knitting out of the air. He slithered it through his fingers. He laid it against his tattooed cheek. He kissed it.

'It doesn't hurt me,' he said. 'It makes me feel better. It puts a spring in my step. It lights up my life. It gives me strength.'

And Amy saw it was true. Granite was sitting up straighter. His black eyes burned with a greedy light. He smiled broadly.

'It's what the Twig made, isn't it? I knew she could. Of course she could. Like Amber. Like her mother. Gorgeous. Awesome. Glorious *gold*!'

28

An Emerald Green Rat

Amy had a strong urge to run. So she did.

Down the spiral stairs, past the empty rooms. Past the hideous cross-eyed, hook-nosed, pointy-eared stone gargoyles, with their accusing eyes. Never again, she told herself. I'll never, ever make them like that. Whatever Aunt Agnes says, I won't do it. I'll make nice statues if I have to make anything. I'll do angels with sweet faces. Puppy dogs and fluffy cats and everything NICE!

No more spoiling.

She reached her room. She knew that she would have to leave it. Leave everything. My lovely chamber, my princess room, she thought, but who wants it? Not me, not now.

She laid the dead white rat out on her bedcover. She stroked his little paws. She wiped the blood gently from his nose.

215

'I even spoiled you,' she whispered. 'I'm sorry. You were the best. Sweet rat dreams.'

She needed a coffin for him. The jewellery box was just the thing. She tipped the rings and necklaces out and placed the rat gently on the yellow velvet inside. She planned to give him a proper burial when she could. She packed a few things into a bag.

Amy went downstairs. There was no one about. Not even any Rockers. How was she going to get to the station and make her way home?

Then she heard footsteps. A female rockgoyle appeared from the Reception Chamber. *Deception Chamber*. That first rockgoyle had been right.

It was the female rockgoyle that Amy had given the blue cloak to. She knew it was because she was still wearing it.

'What's in that box?' asked the rockgoyle. 'Precious things I think, by the way you're clutching it?'

'Yes,' said Amy. She undid the catch and opened the lid. 'My rat. Shane Annigan killed my white rat.'

'So I see. No name for the white rat, eh? We all deserve a name.'

'I...I don't – Oh, that's another thing I've done wrong. I'm so hopeless! What's your name?'

'Petal. Does it suit me?' She giggled. 'You're not hopeless, there's always hope. Try your friend in the germinating compost.'

Amy stared at her. 'But he's dead.'

'And the gargoyles were never alive!' Petal grinned.

'Oh, yes, that's true ... Will you come with me? I'm scared.'

Petal fingered her blue cloak and smiled. 'Why not?' They both took a lantern and made their way down to the underground caverns.

'I'm sorry I wasn't nice to you,' Amy said as she and the rockgoyle hurried along the corridors.

'Good,' said Petal. 'I'm sorry I wasn't nice to you too. I've heard you're not going to make any bad rockgoyles any more. I'm glad.'

They came to the room with the pond and lit the lanterns. Amy quickly took the white rat from the box and handed him to the rockgoyle. 'You do it . . . Please.'

Petal took the limp body in her stubby, clawed fingers. She stroked his white snout. 'Come back to us, Rat,' she whispered. She settled him carefully in the net and let him sink into the green soupy mixture. 'The rat might come out a bit different. You'll be ready for that? The compost is very strong.' She paused. 'Can you bear that? What if he is as ugly as me, hey? The ugliest rat in the whole world, then what?'

'I'll still love him and he'll still be my best friend,' said Amy.

They stood side by side while Petal swung the net gently from side to side in the compost. The green liquid popped and exploded with smelly green gas.

'Is anything happening? Is he coming back?'

'Hush. Wait,' said Petal.

Suddenly Petal snatched up the net and lifted it free. She turned to the sink and quickly ran a torrent of water over it.

'What are you doing?' cried Amy. 'Is he all right?'

217

She pushed round Petal to get a look. 'Rat? Rat? He isn't moving. He's gone green!'

The rat had been dyed emerald green. His nose had elongated into a very long snout and his tail curled like a corkscrew.

'As green as the furzz trees!' laughed Petal.

'But is he alive?' cried Amy. She snatched the rat up. He was limp in her hands. Then suddenly she felt a pulse begin to thump and his whiskers flickered.

'Pss pss squeak!' said the the rat. He opened his green eyes and grinned a green smile.

The ugly green rat crawled up Amy's arm. He ducked his head beneath her chin and rubbed against her, purring.

'Thank you, Petal,' said Amy. 'That's the best thing anyone's ever done for me. And he's the best rat in the entire Universe.'

Petal led Amy back up to the ground floor. She took her to the sledge store. They chose a small, old sledge and dragged it out. Amy fastened her bags to it.

'I shall be going downhill most of the way,' said Amy. She tried to remember where the station was. 'I'll be fine on my own. I can pull it myself if I need to.'

'Goodbye, Amethyst,' said the rockgoyle. 'I hope you find everything you deserve.'

Amy waved goodbye.

She gazed wistfully at the path that led towards the forest and Wolfgang's hut. No, she thought. Not for me.

She went in the opposite direction, downhill towards the station. She felt sure she'd soon see the railway lines and then she would be sure to find the station.

Amy had made a little nest for the rat by turning her woolly hat upside down and wedging it on the sledge. The rat sat inside it, watching. He looked very comical being so green.

'I'm going home again, Rat. Not rich. Not a princess. No longer a spoiler.'

'Eeek.'

'Yes, but I do have you, don't I, Rat? And now I've thought of a name for you. Furzz. Like the trees that Boldly Seer eats. Do you like it?'

The rat purred.

They came to the first big slope. Amy perched on the sledge and whooshed down it. It was glorious. She loved the snow, she loved the white, the cold; she loved everything about the mountains.

And she had to leave.

'Kwaark! Kwaark!' She looked up. It was Casimir, the great snow seagull, flying straight towards her.

The bird circled round twice then swooped down and landed on her sledge. It eyed her sideways from its beady eyes. Its orange feet flip-flapped as it twirled round on the end of her sledge. It fluffed out its feathers and tucked in its wings. It didn't look hostile. It looked positively friendly.

'What is it?' Amy said. 'A message?'

Something like fizzy wine began to course through her veins. Something like hope, like happiness, sparkled and popped inside her. Could it be a message from Copper?

219

Dear, Dear Amy,

We are safely back at Squitcher's village. It's jolly jolly cold! Boldly Seer brought us. Questrid and Wolfgang are fine – it was a lie about the poison cobweb. Wolfgang is a bit cross because he's got to walk all the way back and he says the wolves will be hungry and missing him.

Hope Casimir finds you.

Thank you for everything you did to help. You are a great friend. Please, please come back to Spindle House to us, or if that's too Woody, the Rock. You'd love Ruby, and she'd love you. Amber says you must come.

You'll never find the station on your own.

Thank you for all you've done. I miss you already. Come soon. Love from your <u>friend</u>.

Copper. xxx

Amy kissed the green rat on his green nose.

The seagull rose up, spread his wings and set off for home. Amy turned the sledge round and followed him. He would lead her back to Spindle House and her friends.

She was going home too.